She felt her robe slip from her shoulders, and pool at her feet.

His lips were cool and fresh, exploring hers with a kind of exquisite, lingering deliberation.

Tara felt herself sigh against his mouth, a deep-drawn breath held for an eternity. As she descended into the sweet chaos of pure sensation, she told herself, somehow, that she should hold back—walk away. That this was wrong because Adam belonged to someone else, and it could only lead to heartbreak.

But it had been so long since she'd known what it was to be a woman. After Jack's betrayal, she'd believed herself armored forever against the seductive craving of the flesh, but it was only a fragile shell, after all, and soon shattered. All it had taken was Adam—*Adam....*

SARA CRAVEN was born in South Devon, England, and surrounded by books, grew up in a house by the sea. After leaving school she worked as a local journalist, covering everything from flower shows to murders. She started writing for Harlequin in 1975. Apart from writing, her passions include films, music, cooking and eating in good restaurants. She now lives in Somerset.

Sara Craven has recently become the latest—and last ever—winner of the U.K. quiz show "Mastermind."

Books by Sara Craven

HARLEQUIN PRESENTS®
1901—DECEIVED
1944—ONE RECKLESS NIGHT
1963—ULTIMATE TEMPTATION
1999—A NANNY FOR CHRISTMAS

SARA CRAVEN

The Seduction Game

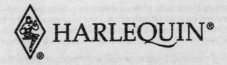

TORONTO • NEW YORK • LONDON
AMSTERDAM • PARIS • SYDNEY • HAMBURG
STOCKHOLM • ATHENS • TOKYO • MILAN • MADRID
PRAGUE • WARSAW • BUDAPEST • AUCKLAND

ISBN 0-373-12030-3

THE SEDUCTION GAME

First North American Publication 1999.

CHAPTER ONE

As the intercom buzzer sounded Tara Lyndon reached across, without taking her eyes from the computer screen in front of her, and flicked a switch.

'Janet?' Her tone was pleasant but crisp. 'I thought I said no interruptions.'

'I'm sorry, Miss Lyndon.' Her secretary's tone was rueful. 'But your sister's on the line, and she's not easy to refuse.'

Don't I know it? Tara thought with an inward sigh, anticipating the purpose of Becky's call.

Aloud, she said, 'OK, Janet, put her through, please.'

'Darling.' Becky's tone lilted along the line. 'How are you? Isn't the weather glorious?'

'We're both fine,' Tara said drily. 'Becky, I'm up to my eyes in work. Can you make it snappy, please?'

'No problem.' Her sister's response was too swift and too mild. 'I was just calling to check on the arrangements for the weekend. I couldn't remember exactly what we'd agreed.'

Pinocchio, thought Tara, your nose has just grown another two inches.

'There's no great confusion,' she returned. 'You invited me down to Hartside. I told you I couldn't make it.'

'And I told you to think it over,' was the immediate reply. 'So have you?'

Tara closed her eyes. 'Becky, it's very kind of you, but I have things of my own to do.'

'Don't tell me. You're flying to Dusseldorf to interview someone who might be perfect for a job in Tokyo.'

'No,' Tara said. 'I'm going away for a complete break. Total rest and relaxation,' she added, surreptitiously testing the length of her own nose.

'But you could have that with us,' Becky wheedled. 'If this weather holds up, we'll be using the pool. And the garden's looking wonderful. Besides, the children are always asking where you are these days.'

'Nonsense,' Tara said sternly. 'Giles and Emma probably wouldn't recognise me if they roller-bladed over my recumbent body.'

'Exactly what I'm getting at,' Becky came back at her immediately. 'You're so tied up in that career of yours that none of us ever see you. And with Ma and Pa nearly on the other side of the world—I—I miss you, Sis.'

The throb of pathos sounded almost convincing, Tara thought, amused in spite of herself, until, of course, one remembered Becky's adoring husband Harry, her ebullient but delightful brats, her endlessly kind and supportive in-laws and the village of Hartside where she pretty well reigned as queen. If her sister spent one lonely moment, it would be through her own choice.

Interpreting Tara's silence as an implicit weakening of her position, Becky went on eagerly, 'Darling, it's been ages since you came down. Surely you could spare me a couple of days.'

'And if I did,' Tara said slowly, 'could you swear to

me that you haven't rounded up yet another unfortunate man to run past me as a potential husband.'

'Oh, for heaven's sake,' her sister said airily. 'I wrote you off as a lost cause a long time ago.'

'Becky.'

'You're so suspicious,' her elder complained.

'With very good reason,' Tara said grimly. 'All right, who is he?'

'My goodness,' Becky said with asperity. 'It's come to something when I can't invite a new neighbour round for a drink without you going into conspiracy theory mode.'

'Who—is—he?' Tara repeated through gritted teeth.

Becky sighed. 'He's just moved into Glebe Cottage—that lovely place near the church. He's a tax lawyer, middle thirties, and very attractive.'

'And still single?' Tara's brows lifted. 'What's the matter with him?'

'There's nothing the matter,' Becky defended. 'They're extremely nice people.'

'They?'

Becky hesitated. 'Well, his mother's staying with him at the moment, helping him settle in.'

'My God.' Tara felt an unholy bubble of glee well up inside her. 'He's thirty-something and he still lives with Mummy?'

'Nothing of the kind. It's a purely temporary measure. She has a very nice home of her own. And she's desperate for him to meet the right woman.'

'I'm sure she is.' Tara's tone was dry. 'She probably has the poisoned dagger ready and waiting.'

'I don't think that job is doing you any good,' Becky said severely. 'It's made you disagreeably cynical.'

'It's certainly taught me to differentiate between people's public faces and private agendas,' Tara agreed. 'Whatever, I'm afraid I'm not tempted to change my plans. I'm going to spend the weekend relaxing in my own way.' Not to mention the following two weeks as well, she added silently.

'And on your own, I suppose?'

There was something about the question that flicked Tara on the raw. 'Not necessarily.'

'Tara,' Becky shrieked. 'You mean you've actually met someone. Tell me everything.'

'No,' Tara said, already regretting that she'd allowed herself to be provoked into the fib. 'There isn't anything to tell. Not yet.' Which was no more than the truth, she placated her conscience.

'You slyboots,' Becky said gleefully. 'You've got to give me a hint. Is he tall or short? Dark or fair?'

'No comment.'

'But he is gorgeous, right?' Becky persisted. 'And with money?'

Tara sighed. 'It's a pity they did away with the Spanish Inquisition, Beck. I could have got you in at the top level, no problem.'

'Naturally I'm going to be interested,' her sister said with dignity. 'Do you realise how long it is since you had even a marginal involvement with a man?'

'Only too well,' Tara said gently. 'And why.'

'Well, it's time you put all that behind you,' Becky said firmly, after a pause. 'I've been telling you for ages that not all men are rats. Let's hope this weekend is a step in the right direction.'

A vision rose in front of Tara's eyes of a sunlit creek, a boat's mast dark against the bright water. A square white house set amidst trees, and no sound except the cry of birds.

Involuntarily her mouth curled. 'Oh, I think I can promise that. Now I must go, Becky. I have a report to finish.'

'And you're not going to give me even a teensy idea what your new man is like—so that I can tell Harry.'

'Just say that it's early days. He'll understand.'

'Yes,' said Harry's loving wife, with something of a snap. 'I expect he will.'

Tara was laughing as she put the phone down, yet it wasn't really funny, she thought ruefully. She should have stuck to her guns. Admitted that she was going to spend her holiday alone, and what the hell. But Becky's assumption that this had to be the case had riled her for some reason. And it would also have provided her sister with extra ammunition in her bid to persuade her down to Hartside, she reminded herself defensively.

Becky could not be allowed to organise her life as if she was some extension of the carol concert, or the village fête. Or continue to dangle allegedly eligible bachelors in front of her, not to mention the occasional divorcé, or, in dire straits, widower.

Yet it was still genuinely stupid to let her think there's a new man in my life, she told herself. Beck won't leave it there. She's like a ferret. Thank God she doesn't realise where I'm going. She'll assume I'm jetting off somewhere for sun, sangria and sex—as I used to do with Jack.

Something closed in her mind at the memory. Like a shutter coming down to defend her against pain. Except there was no defence.

Becky was right about one thing, she thought. It was more than time to let go. To release herself from the dead hand of the past. And maybe a new relationship was what she needed to help the healing process along.

But, like a burned child, she'd hung back from the fire, letting the demands of her career fill the aching space that Jack had left. And now perhaps it was too late.

She pushed her chair back restlessly, rising to walk over to the picture window behind her, staring out at the vista of City offices which confronted her. This was what was important. This was what mattered, she told herself. She was a partner in a top recruitment service— a headhunter who could smell the blood in the water. Too busy setting executive traps to offer any personal bait herself.

As she turned away, she glimpsed her reflection in the glass and halted. Scrutinised what she took for granted each day—the mid-brown hair, immaculately bobbed just short of shoulder-length, the white silk shirt, buttoned to the throat, topping the dark skirt ending discreetly on the knee. Neat, efficient and unthreatening.

An image which she'd actively sought, and now, suddenly, found vaguely unsatisfying.

Oh, for heaven's sake, she apostrophised herself impatiently. You must need a holiday more than you thought.

She sat down and applied herself with new determination to her report, scanning swiftly through what she'd already written.

Tom Fortescue had come highly recommended, she thought. He was well-qualified, and a man in a hurry. And yet...

Tara shook her head. Her usually reliable antennae seemed to be sounding a warning, and she didn't understand why.

There were no significant gaps in his CV, and he'd interviewed well. She had nothing to go on but sheer intuition. And that intuition was telling her not to suggest Mr Fortescue for the highly paid position at Bearcroft Holdings for which he seemed so eminently suited.

Her doubts were there, loud and clear, in every line of her report. On the surface, it was a dispassionate, professional assessment, but Tara could see she'd been non-committal where she should have been enthusiastic, guarded when she should have been singing his praises. She sighed and saved the file to disk.

It would be up to her associates to make the final judgement, of course, and in some ways she was glad she would not be there to justify her assessment. Or to express any regrets to Tom Fortescue, who would not be pleased to find himself sidelined on her say-so. He was sharp and ambitious, and he'd come to Marchant Southern specifically because he wanted to fill the Bearcroft spot, and Tara was sure he regarded the appointment as in the bag.

But by the time she came back from leave the dust should have settled, she told herself philosophically. And Mr Fortescue could advance his career with another firm of headhunters.

She retrieved the disk from her machine, and went out to give it to Janet. And checked, registering with shock the figure perched with easy familiarity on the edge of her secretary's desk.

'Good afternoon.' Tom Fortescue got up, smiling, and walked to meet her. 'I happened to be in the area, and wondered if you'd like to have lunch?'

In a pig's ear, Tara thought cynically. She'd never given him the slightest hint that she'd be prepared to meet him socially. But that hadn't stopped him. No doubt he intended to pump her discreetly for her verdict in some convenient wine bar.

'Rather too obvious, my boy,' she advised him under her breath, rigidly conscious of the disk in her hand.

Her answering smile was cool. 'I'm sorry. I go on leave this afternoon, and I need to clear my desk. I'm going to make do with the sandwich service.'

'I'm sorry, too.' He paused, pulling a face. 'But I'm sure there'll be other opportunities.'

When hell freezes over, thought Tara, feeling obliged to walk with him to the lift and chat civilly while they waited for it to arrive.

Altogether too sure of himself, she thought as she walked back. And how dared he think her such easy game?

Janet, however, was looking wistful.

'He was lovely,' she confided. 'I told him you were busy, and he said he was happy to wait.'

'I hope he maintains that philosophical attitude,' Tara said drily, as she passed over the disk. 'Sign the letters in my absence, please, Jan.' She paused. 'And mark that report "Confidential", circulating it to associates only. It won't be wanted until Tuesday morning's meeting.'

'Will do.' Janet smiled cheerfully up at her. 'What time are you going?'

'I'd like to be away by two. I still have some packing to do.'

'Are you going somewhere gorgeous?'

'I think so,' Tara agreed. 'And do you know the best thing about it?'

'What?' Jan's eyes widened. She clearly expected she was going to be told about George Clooney's favourite hideaway.

Tara leaned towards her confidentially. 'No phone,' she whispered, and went back, laughing, to her office.

'Polish,' Tara muttered to herself, checking the items in the box in front of her. 'Stuff for the brass and silver, oven cleaner, washing-up liquid, and rubber gloves.' She nodded her satisfaction, and tucked a packet of cleaning clothes around the cans to keep them steady.

Melusine, sleek, black, green-eyed and openly glum as she'd observed the packing process, had taken up a position on the table beside the box. Now she reached out a delicate paw and swiped at the plastic wrapping round the packet.

'It's all right.' Tara ran a caressing hand over the silky fur. 'You're coming with me.' That's if I can get you in your basket, she added silently.

Melusine preferred to travel on the front passenger seat, with her paws on the dashboard, free, untrammelled, and with an excellent view. At least until her path was crossed by a police car, ambulance or fire engine, when the sound of the siren would cause her to wrap herself round Tara's neck like a scarf.

Her special bowl, her bean bag, and the cat food she favoured at the moment were already in the boot of the car. The basket was hidden behind the living-room sofa, waiting for the psychological moment when she could be tricked inside.

In fact, Tara had bestowed far less thought on the contents of her own travel bag, she realised with amusement. Apart from the usual quota of undies and toiletries, she was only taking jeans, shorts, T-shirts, sweaters, and training shoes that had never seen a designer label. All practical clothing for the job ahead.

Becky would kill me if she knew what I was doing, she thought ruefully as she carried her box of cleaning materials down to the car. *But Ma and Pa will be back next month, and I want the house bright and shining to welcome them.*

She hadn't the slightest doubt that was where they'd head for as soon as they'd unpacked and rested from their South African trip. The house in Chelsea was still nominally home, but Silver Creek House had been their favoured retreat for years now.

It was fairly basic. As well as lacking a telephone, the house had no television or central heating, and the kitchen stove and water heater worked from a large gas tank, sited discreetly at the rear of the house. But these were minor inconveniences as far as Tara was concerned. She'd never minded cleaning out the fireplaces in the sitting room and dining room, or filling the log baskets which fed them. She loved the house, and all its memories of happy family holidays.

During the winter, the Pritchards kept an eye on the place. Mrs Pritchard worked part-time in the nearby village shop, and Mr Pritchard was employed at the small boatyard upstream, where her parents' much loved boat *Naiad* spent the winter.

Mrs Pritchard would have been happy to carry out any cleaning that was needed, but Tara preferred to do it herself. Anomalous as it might seem, it was work she thoroughly enjoyed.

When she and Becky had been younger, it had been her sister who'd been the potential high-flyer—the girl about town with the high-paid job and crowded social life. Tara had always been the quieter, more domesticated one.

No one could believe it when Becky met Harry, and opted for marriage and motherhood without even a backward glance at all she was giving up.

However, no one could pretend that housework would ever be Becky's forte, Tara thought affectionately. But by bringing the same organisational skills to marriage as she had to her career she'd safely ensured she'd never have to do any.

It would be inconceivable to Becky that anyone would give up precious holiday time to scrub, polish and add the odd lick of paint to a shabby, elderly house. And equally incredible that the same person might actually revel in their self-appointed task, or find it positively therapeutic.

Tara glimpsed herself in the mirror as she finally headed for the door, cat basket in hand and a furious Melusine giving her a piece of her mind. Marchant Southern would have got the shock of their lives if they could see her now, she thought, grinning as she surveyed her faded denim skirt topped by an ancient sweatshirt. Her hair was bundled up into a baseball cap, and her bare feet were thrust into a pair of canvas slip-ons which had seen better days.

But what the hell? she thought as she locked up and went down to the car. I'm not going to be seeing anyone unless I choose. After all, there isn't another house within miles.

Or at least another inhabited house, she amended quickly. Which Dean's Mooring certainly wasn't. Up to three years ago it had been occupied by old Ambrose Dean, white-bearded and fierce, a loner who had guarded his privacy jealously. After his death, the cottage, which stood about a hundred yards upstream from Silver Creek House, had remained empty, and was fast becoming derelict.

Ambrose had been a bachelor, and apparently had had no living relatives. Certainly no one ever came to see him. Jim Lyndon, Tara's father, had spoken vaguely of contacting the lawyers dealing with the old man's estate and perhaps making an offer for the cottage, but had never actually got around to doing anything constructive about it.

Maybe I will, Tara thought idly as she started out of London. After all, the parents won't want to find themselves living next to an eyesore. And I've nothing

booked in my diary but some serious peace and quiet.
I could, maybe, start the ball rolling.

On the other hand, I could forget about everything
that smacks of business and just—chill out. What utter
bliss.

But the road to paradise was not an easy one, she
soon discovered. Other people had also decided to
make an early start to the Bank Holiday weekend, and
traffic was grindingly heavy.

By the time Tara turned the car on to the rutted track
which led to the house her head was aching, and
Melusine was expressing vigorous disapproval from the
rear seat.

She parked in the yard at the back and got out,
stretching luxuriously and drinking in gulps of the cool
early evening air. Then she reached into her bag and
found the key.

The house felt chill and slightly damp as she stepped
into the kitchen. There was a strange mustiness in the
atmosphere too.

The smell of loneliness, Tara thought, looking
around her. I'll soon change that.

As usual, there was a box of groceries waiting on
the scrubbed table, courtesy of Mrs Pritchard, and one
of her magnificent steak and kidney pies covered by a
teatowel resting beside it. Tucked under it was a note,
stating that the gas tank was full and the log man had
delivered the previous week, together with the various
invoices for these services. And, waiting in the big old
fridge, was a bottle of Tara's favourite Chablis.

Already she could feel the stresses and strains of the

past weeks easing away, she thought, heaving a sigh of pure satisfaction.

Mrs Pritchard, you're an angel, she told her silently.

She went back to the car, sniffing at the tubs of lavender that her mother had planted the previous year, and collected the frantic Melusine, who gave her a filthy look and stormed up the clematis-hung trellis on to the shed roof.

'Feel free,' Tara told her as she unloaded the rest of her things from the car and carried them into the house. From past experience, Melusine would sulk until supper time, then appear as if nothing had happened, twining herself affectionately round Tara's legs.

When the entire family was staying Tara contented herself with a small room at the back, but now she had the luxury of choice, and she opted for the large room at the front, which matched that of her parents, just across the landing. She might not be spending much time on the river—even the most cursory inspection downstairs confirmed she had plenty to do—but she could enjoy the view, and let the sound of the water lull her to sleep at night.

She tossed her travel bag on to the wide bed and walked to the window, flinging back the half-drawn curtains and opening the casement to take her first long look at the creek itself.

And stopped in utter astonishment and swiftly mounting anger. She'd expected the usual tranquil expanse of water, ruffled only by moorhens or a passing duck, with *Naiad* as a centrepiece.

Instead she was confronted by another boat, a large

cabin cruiser, smart, glossy, and shouting money. And tied up, for pity's sake, at *their* landing stage.

She said aloud, furiously, 'What the hell…?' and halted, her attention suddenly riveted by the loud, excited barking of a dog just below the window, and Melusine's answering yowl of fright.

'*No*,' Tara exploded. She was across the room in two strides, and flying down the stairs, dragging back the bolts on the front door with hands that shook with rage as well as fear for her pet.

She hurled herself outside, colliding heavily as she did so with another body, much taller and more muscular than her own. Was aware, shockingly, of bare, hair-roughened skin grazing her cheek. Heard a man's deep voice say, 'Ouch,' and felt strong hands steadying her.

'Let go of me.' She tore herself free. 'My cat—where is she?'

'She's safe. She's roosting in that tree over there.'

Swinging round, Tara saw Melusine crouching on a branch twenty feet from the ground. And, leaping joyously below, still barking, a golden Labrador dog, not long out of puppyhood.

'Oh, that's great,' she said savagely. 'That's just bloody wonderful. Call your damned dog off, will you? And when you've got him under control, the pair of you can clear out. This is a private landing.'

'But apparently not a happy one.' The interloper's faint drawl was composed, even amused. All she could see of him was a dark shape between herself and the setting sun. She took a step backwards, shading her eyes.

She registered dark blond hair, in need of cutting, and cool blue eyes. A strong face, with a beaky nose, high cheekbones, and a firm, humorous mouth above a jutting chin. Not conventionally handsome by any means, but searingly attractive, she thought with a shock of recognition. He had a good body, too, lean and tanned, and clothed only from the waist down in faded denim which emphasised his long legs and flat stomach.

She felt a sudden sensuous tingle quivering along her nerve-endings that she had not experienced since Jack. And she resented it. More than that, feared it.

Dry-mouthed, she hurried into speech. 'There's not much to be happy about. You're trespassing, and your dog has tried to kill my cat.'

'Dogs chase cats. That's a fact of life. They rarely if ever catch them. That's another. And if he did get near I wouldn't give much for his chances.'

His laconic drawl was infuriating. He turned towards the Labrador, put two fingers in his mouth to utter a piercing whistle, and called, 'Buster.' The dog came instantly to his side, eyes sparkling with excitement and tail wagging.

Tara glared at them both.

'And what chance does my cat have—stuck there in that tree?'

'Is she really stuck?' he asked mildly. 'I can probably do something about that.'

Tara took a deep breath. 'The only thing that you can do is go. You've no right to be here. If you weren't trespassing, none of this would have happened.'

'And just what are your rights in all this?'

Tara jerked a thumb. 'That happens to be my house.'

'Really?' The straight brows lifted. 'Now I could have sworn it belonged to a Jim and Barbara Lyndon, who are both in their fifties and currently in South Africa. I must have been misinformed.'

'They're my parents.' His easy assurance was unnerving. 'And may I ask how you came by this information?'

He shrugged. 'People in the village are very helpful.' He paused. 'So it's not really your house at all.' It was a statement rather than a question.

Tara gritted her teeth. 'If you want to split hairs...'

'An excellent idea,' he agreed affably. 'You see, I was also told that this landing was a shared one with Dean's Mooring.'

'Back in the mists of time, perhaps.' She hated the defensive note in her voice. 'However, Mr Dean never used it. He didn't even have a boat.'

'Ah,' he said softly. 'But, you see, I have. And as clearly no one is using the Dean's Mooring share at the moment, I'm borrowing it.'

'But you can't—not without permission from the owner,' she protested wildly.

'And do you know how to contact him?' He was grinning openly now.

Tara could have ground her teeth. 'Hardly,' she returned stiffly. 'As I'm sure you're already aware, Mr Dean died some time ago.'

'Ah,' he said. 'And I left the ouija board in my other jeans. Well, they say possession is nine tenths of the law, so it looks as if we're going to be neighbours.'

'But you can't just—move in and take over like this.'

'The evidence suggests I can—and I have. So why don't we work out a co-existence pact.'

Because I don't want you here, she thought. It's too lonely—too remote to share with some passing stranger. And because you worry me in ways I don't understand.

She hurried into speech. 'You must see that's impossible. You could be anybody.'

'On the lines of escaped criminal, rapist or axe murderer, I presume.' He gave her a weary look. 'Would you like to see my driving licence—my gold card?'

'The only thing I'd like to see is you and your boat sailing away,' Tara said inimically. 'There's a marina about six miles upstream. You should find everything you need there.'

'I think it's a little premature to be discussing my needs,' he drawled. 'Besides, I'm quite contented where I am. And, as I was here first, maybe it's you that should be moving on. But I won't make an issue of it,' he added kindly. 'You're welcome to stay as long as you don't play loud music or throw wild parties. I like my peace and quiet.'

For a moment she couldn't move or speak. Her eyes blazed into his—fire meeting ice. Then, with a small, inarticulate sound, she marched back to the house and went in, slamming the door behind her with such violence that a blue and white plate fell off the wall and smashed at her feet.

'Oh, *hell*,' said Tara, and, to her own surprise and disgust, burst into tears.

CHAPTER TWO

'MELUSINE.' Perched on an inadequate pair of steps, Tara held out a coaxing handful of meaty snacks. 'Come on, darling.'

But Melusine only gave her a baleful glance, and continued to hang on to the precarious safety of her branch.

Tara groaned inwardly. She'd hoped against hope that Melusine would rescue herself somehow, but her pet clearly had other ideas. She wouldn't climb down, and it was physically impossible for Tara to reach her.

Which left a drive to the village and a phone call to either the fire service or the local RSPCA, she thought despondently.

Nothing, but nothing, was going according to plan.

However, that still didn't excuse or explain the pathetic bout of crying she'd indulged in earlier, she reminded herself. She didn't usually walk away from confrontations, or behave like a wimp afterwards.

I handled the whole thing so badly, she thought, as if I'd forgotten every management skill I ever learned. But he caught me off-guard. Put me at a disadvantage.

But now, face washed, drops in her reddened eyes, and a modicum of blusher judiciously applied, she was back, firing on all cylinders. If she could just get Melusine down from this tree...

'Having problems?'

The sudden sound of her adversary's voice behind

23

her made her jump. The steps lurched and Tara cried out, grabbing at the trunk of the tree in front of her.

'Do you have to creep up on me?' she snarled as she steadied herself.

'It wasn't intentional,' he said. 'I could see she wouldn't budge, so I came to help. You need a longer ladder.'

'Full marks for observation,' Tara said between her teeth as she descended from the steps. The tatty jeans, she saw, had now been topped by an equally ancient checked shirt with a tear in one sleeve. 'Unfortunately, this is as good as it gets.'

'Not necessarily.'

She gave him a caustic look. 'You have a ladder stashed on board your boat? How unusual.'

'Not on board,' he said. 'But I noticed one earlier in an outhouse behind the cottage.'

'You certainly haven't been wasting your time.' Tara felt cold suddenly. 'And what about the contents of the cottage itself? Have you made an inventory of those too?'

'I've had a look round.' He nodded. 'Don't tell me you've never been tempted. Especially,' he added pointedly, 'as I believe you have a key.'

Tara flushed, silently damning the kindly but eager tongues in the village. 'That's for security purposes. I don't pry into other people's business,' she added, lifting her chin.

Although she *had* been in Dean's Mooring, her conscience reminded her. After Mr Dean's death, she'd helped her mother clear out what little food there'd been, and strip and burn the bedding he'd used. Amid the squalor, there'd been several nice pieces of furniture, she recalled uneasily. Things which could easily tempt someone for whom honesty wasn't a major factor.

'Then you must be a saint.' He paused. 'But you don't seem to be working any miracles where your cat's concerned, so shall I fetch that ladder?'

She wanted to tell him to go to hell, and stuff his ladder where the sun didn't shine, but discretion suggested a more conciliatory approach. After all, she didn't want to spend the night at the foot of a tree, wooing an unresponsive cat.

'Thank you,' she said unsmilingly.

'God, how that must have hurt,' he said mockingly, and set off towards Dean's Mooring.

Frowningly, she watched him go, broad-shouldered and narrow-hipped, covering the ground with his long, lithe stride. No matter how grave her doubts about him, she could not deny he possessed a lethal physical attraction. Which was not the kind of thing she needed to notice, she thought, biting her lip.

Her safest course might indeed be to pack up and return to London. Or even go down to Becky's, she reminded herself without enthusiasm.

But that would leave her parents' house defenceless, as well as Dean's Mooring. Knowing that she was there, able to keep an eye on both properties, might prompt him to cut his losses and depart. If, indeed, he was there to steal.

She couldn't believe he had just stumbled on Silver Creek by accident. On the contrary, he appeared to have done his homework thoroughly.

But the shabby clothes and generally unkempt appearance—at least two days' growth of stubble, she'd noticed disapprovingly—didn't match the glamorous cruiser. Unless he'd stolen that too, of course.

People with boats like that tended to enjoy showing them off on the broader stretches of the river. Mixing with others in a similar income bracket. So he must have a reason for hiding himself away in this secluded corner.

All in all, he was an enigma, and someone she could well do without. But he couldn't be driven away. That was already more than clear.

Maybe sheer boredom and the total lack of amenities would do the trick in the end, and all she needed was patience.

I can only hope, she thought, sighing, as she watched him return, the ladder balanced effortlessly on his shoulder.

She watched him set it against the tree and wedge it securely, then stepped forward. 'You'd better let me go up for her. She's not very good with strangers.'

'I wonder where she learned that,' he murmured, his mouth slanting. 'All the same...'

He put his foot on the bottom rung, and started to climb.

Melusine watched his approach, back hunched.

He'd either be scratched or totally ignored, Tara thought, smouldering with annoyance at his high-handed performance. And either would be more than acceptable to her. Serve him right for being an arrogant swine.

He reached the branch, stretched out a hand, and made a soft chirruping sound.

And Melusine, treacherous bloody animal that she was, rose gracefully, picked her way towards him, and jumped lightly on to his shoulder.

He murmured to her soothingly, then descended

swiftly and competently, bending slightly so that Tara could retrieve her purring feline.

'I have to thank you again,' she said, her voice so wooden she could have spat splinters.

'I'm sure it won't become a habit,' he returned. He scratched gently under Melusine's chin, which she arched ecstatically to accommodate him. 'She's friendlier than you give her credit for.'

'Not usually.'

He grinned again, the cool blue gaze looking her over with unashamed appraisal. 'Then she's like most women—contrary.'

'And you're like most men—sexist,' Tara shot back at him.

'Guilty as charged,' he said cheerfully. 'I believe in two genders, and thank God for each and every difference between them. But it doesn't make me a bad person,' he added his eyes fixed on the swift tightening of Tara's mouth. 'So, what's her name?'

'Melusine,' she said curtly.

'A witch name,' he said musingly, then laughed softly. 'Now, why does that not surprise me?' He stroked the cat's glossy head with his forefinger. 'How do you do, my proud beauty? I'm Adam Barnard. And I hope you're none the worse for your ordeal.'

Adam Barnard. Tara felt the name stir in her mind with something like pleasure.

She hurriedly covered her involuntary reaction with waspishness. 'You'd better leave the ladder where it is. When your dog gets loose, Melusine will be back up the tree again, looking for sanctuary.'

'I may join her.' His tone was grim, the tanned mobile face suddenly austere as he looked her over. 'Did no one ever tell you the Cold War is over?'

Tara's lips tightened. 'I didn't come down to play good neighbours.'

'Just as well.' He shrugged. 'Clearly you'd be lousy at it. As a matter of interest, why are you here looking for splendid isolation?' The blue eyes quizzed her. 'Hiding from something?'

'Certainly not.' Tara returned his gaze levelly. 'I came to do some work on the house. It's a while since anyone's been here, and I don't want it falling into rack and ruin...'

'Like Dean's Mooring,' he suggested.

'Yes, actually. I think it's a tragedy to leave the place abandoned like that, with no one to care for it.'

'Is that what the previous owner did? Cared?'

There was an odd note in his voice.

'I—I don't know,' Tara said defensively. 'I didn't know Mr Dean very well. No one did. He hardly ever went out, and no one came to see him. Even when he was ill he wouldn't have the doctor, or the district nurse. But I suppose he was happy in his own way.'

'Keeping himself to himself.' He nodded reflectively. 'It seems to be catching.'

Tara bit her lip in annoyance. Her arms must have tightened on Melusine too, because the cat began to wriggle.

'I'd better take her indoors,' she said quickly. 'Well—as I said—thank you.'

'Is that all?'

'I beg your pardon?'

'I was thinking you could offer me some rather more—tangible form of gratitude.' The blue eyes watched her coolly, consideringly, lingering, it seemed, on the curve of her mouth.

She felt a shiver of tension curl down her spine.

She'd been a fool to hang around out here, allowing him to needle her, she thought grimly. She should have stuck with cold and dismissive, and got the hell out of it.

She took a step backwards, trying to be casual. 'I've already been as grateful as I'm likely to get.'

'Are you quite sure about that?' He sounded faintly amused.

She thought longingly of her mobile phone, in a desk drawer at her flat in London.

'Convinced,' she said curtly. 'Now you must excuse me.'

If she made it to the front door, she promised herself, she would walk straight through the house, grabbing her bag and Melusine's basket on the way, out through the back entrance, into her car and off. Destination unknown and unimportant.

'That's a shame,' he said softly. 'You see, for the past hour I've been having these amazing fantasies, and you're the only one who can fulfill them.'

She must have heard the words 'her blood ran cold' hundreds of times, without beginning to guess what it could feel like to have ice crawling below the surface of her skin. But she knew now. Felt the ache of it paralyse her. Stultify her reasoning.

'So, Miss Tara Lyndon.' His voice was barely above a whisper. 'Are you going to make all my dreams come true?'

'When hell freezes over.' Her tone was ragged, but she lifted her chin and stared at him with contempt and antagonism. Maybe if she defied him, let him see she was no one's push-over, he'd back off.

He sighed. 'I was afraid of that. Mrs Pritchard will be so disappointed.'

Tara had the curious impression she was involved in some kind of alternative reality. Or had her opponent simply escaped from somewhere?

She said hoarsely, 'What's Mrs Pritchard got to do with anything? And how did you know my name?'

'Well, you can't possibly be Becky. You're not wearing a wedding ring.'

He made himself sound like the voice of sweet reason, Tara thought furiously. Was there any family detail Mrs Pritchard hadn't confided to him?

'And she told me she'd made you one of her steak and kidney pies, because you like them so much,' he went on, then paused. 'I got the impression she thought you might be prepared to share it with me,' he added wistfully. 'And, after all, I did rescue your cat.'

Her lips moved for several seconds before any audible words were formed. Then, 'You—want some steak and kidney pie?' she asked slowly and very carefully. 'Is that what you mean?'

'What else?' His face was solemn, but the blue eyes were dancing in challenge.

Tara wasn't cold any more. She was blazing—burning up with temper. He'd made a total fool of her—reduced her to a shaken mass of insecurity—and there wasn't a thing she could do about it. She couldn't even admit it. And they both knew it.

She swallowed deeply, forcing an approximation of a smile to her rigid mouth.

'Then of course you shall have some.' She shifted the indignant Melusine to look at her watch. 'After all, I wouldn't want to forfeit Mrs Pritchard's good opinion. Shall we say eight o'clock?'

'My God,' he said slowly. 'Under that stony exterior

beats a living heart after all. I'll be counting the
minutes.'

Count away, Tara told him silently. By seven-thirty
both I and my steak and kidney pie will be halfway
back to London. And I won't be coming back until
you're safely out of the picture. You may have charmed
the Pritchards, but I'm not falling for your line. Not
any more. I've been there and done that.

She made herself smile again. 'Well—see you later.'

She walked away without haste, and without looking
back, although she was aware that he was watching her
every step of the way.

Look as much as you want, she thought. It'll be your
last opportunity.

As she closed the front door behind her she realised
she was trembling all over. She halted, trying to steady
her breathing, and Melusine, mewing violently, jumped
from her arms and mooched into the kitchen, whisking
her tail.

Tara went up to her room to retrieve her travel bag.
She couldn't resist a surreptitious peep out of the window, but Adam Barnard was nowhere to be seen. The
ladder had disappeared too, so presumably he was putting it back where he'd found it. He certainly made very
free with other people's property, she thought, fuming.
Well, she couldn't stop him snooping round Dean's
Mooring, perhaps, but she could tip off the local police
about his activities.

And she could find out which estate agency was handling the sale of the property and express the family's
interest in acquiring it. That would deal with unauthor-
ised use of the mooring.

She stared across at the cabin cruiser. What was an
unshaven scruff like Adam Barnard doing in charge of

something so upmarket and glamorous? she wondered uneasily. He couldn't be the owner, yet the boat didn't have the look of a hire craft either.

But for that matter what was he doing here at all—and alone? He didn't give the impression of a man addicted to solitude. And some women—probably flashy blondes—might even find his brand of raffish attraction appealing, she thought, ruthlessly quelling the memory of her own brief, unlooked-for response to him.

Just a slip of the reflexes, she assured herself. And no harm done. Which didn't altogether explain why she was beating such a swift and ignominious retreat.

Tara bit her lip. To run away, of course, would be an open admission that she found him dangerous. That she'd taken his teasing seriously. And that would put her at the far greater risk of appearing an over-reactive and humourless idiot.

Although there was no real reason why she should care what he thought.

And why am I standing here debating the matter, anyway? she demanded vexedly.

Because you haven't been able to pigeon-hole him, said a small voice at the back of her mind. Because so far he's won every round. Because he's a puzzle you can't solve. Not yet.

He'd asked her if she was hiding from something, but she could well have levelled the same question at him. What could possibly have brought him to this secluded patch of river?

Unless, of course, the boat really was stolen, and he really was some kind of criminal.

The thought brought a renewed sense of chill. But, to be fair, he'd hardly made a secret of his presence, she reminded herself. After all, making Mrs Pritchard's acquaintance was tantamount to telling the world.

On the other hand, he could be mounting some terrific double bluff. Making himself so visible and agreeable locally that no one would suspect a thing.

It disturbed her that he'd gained so much background information about her family, and so easily, too. If he was just a passing stranger, what possible use or interest could these details be to him?

Which led her back to the possibility that Adam Barnard did not see Silver Creek simply as a convenient backwater in which to pass a few lazy days.

So, what was his true motivation? And if he was up to no good could she afford to go and leave the house to his tender mercies? Maybe his needling of her had been a deliberate ploy, intended to goad her into flight.

If so, she thought with sudden grim resolution, he's going to be unlucky. Because I won't be driven away, after all. Not before I've found out a little in turn about the so-clever, so-attractive Mr Barnard.

Down in the kitchen, Melusine was sitting huffily by the fridge.

'My poor girl.' Tara ran a caressing hand down her back. 'You've had quite a day. I'd better start making it all up to you, before you walk out on me.'

The Chinese had a curse, she recalled, as she opened a can of tuna and poured milk into a dish. 'May you live in interesting times.'

Certainly the current situation seemed to be quite fascinating enough to fit into that particular frame.

And all she had to do was make sure that the curse did not fall on her. A task well within her capabilities.

But, even as she smiled to herself in quiet confi-

dence, a sudden inner vision of Adam Barnard's tanned
face leapt into her mind.

In one shocked moment Tara saw the mocking twist
of his firm lips, the little devils dancing in his blue eyes,
and wondered if, perhaps, she hadn't bitten off more
than she could chew.

By the time eight o'clock came, Tara felt as if she'd
been stretched on wires. More than once she'd been
tempted to revert to Plan A, and put some serious distance between herself and the enigmatic Mr Barnard.

At the same time she found herself preparing vege-
tables, putting the pie in the oven to reheat, and setting
two places at the kitchen table.

When the bell finally rang, she took a deep breath,
wiped damp palms on her denim-clad hips, and went
to let him in.

For a moment she barely recognised him. He was
clean-shaven, his hair was combed, and the torn jeans
and shirt had been replaced by pale grey trousers and
a black rollneck sweater which looked very like cash-
mere, and he was carrying a bottle of wine.

Nor was he alone. Before Tara could speak, Buster
jumped up at her with a joyous yelp, then squeezed
past and dashed along the passage towards the kitchen.

'Oh, God,' Tara wailed. 'He's after the cat. He'll kill
her.'

'Not a chance.' Adam Barnard laid a detaining hand
on her arm as she prepared to set off in pursuit. 'He's
a young male. It's in his nature to hunt.'

'Then why the hell did you bring him?' She glared
up at him.

'So that they can get things sorted. If they're going
to be neighbours, they need to get along.'

Tara registered that in passing as she freed herself and made for the kitchen. It sounded, she thought with dismay, as if Adam Barnard was planning to stick around for some considerable time.

Then everything else was forgotten as she heard Buster begin to bark excitedly and Melusine's answering and blood-curdling yowl.

'Oh, baby.' Heart thudding, she shot to the rescue. One swift glance from the doorway told her the worst. The dog had Melusine cornered in a small dark space beside the washing machine, and was advancing on her aggressively, barking all the while.

'See what you've done,' she accused Adam Barnard, her voice shaking, as he joined her. 'Call him off.'

'No need,' he said briskly. 'I promise you.'

As Buster lunged forward, a black silk paw came out of the shadows and swiped him across the muzzle. He yelped in pain and surprise and jumped backwards, shaking his head.

'See what I mean.' Adam Barnard's tone was dry. 'The female of any species is always deadlier than any mere male.'

'And I can do without the chauvinist remarks,' Tara snapped. 'She could have been badly hurt.'

'Her nine lives are still intact. Poor old Buster is the one with the bloody nose.' He reached down and scooped up Melusine, who dangled aloofly from his shoulder. 'You big bully,' he scolded softly. 'Give my pup a break.'

Tara saw that the dog was indeed bleeding from a nasty scratch.

'Oh, Lord.' She swallowed. 'I'd better bathe it for him.'

Buster submitted with docility to her ministrations,

his brown eyes full of the soulful anguish of the totally misunderstood.

'That'll teach you,' she muttered as she swabbed the scratch with disinfectant. Melusine watched the process from the safety of the draining board, where she sat, carefully washing the contaminated paw.

'Perhaps I'd better put her in another room,' Tara said as she rinsed her hands.

'Leave them. They'll be fine now that the pecking order has been established.' His mouth curved in amusement. 'You look as if you'd like to banish me to another room as well.'

'It had occurred to me.' Tara gave him a challenging look. 'I'm still not sure why I agreed to this.'

'Oh, I think you probably had an excellent reason,' he said affably. 'But if you're now having second thoughts you could always put my share in a doggy bag, and Buster and I will go back to our lonely boat.'

Her smile was wintry. 'I can probably stand it if you can.' She gestured awkwardly towards the kitchen table. 'Please sit down, and I'll dish up.'

'If you give me a corkscrew, I'll open this.' He held up the wine he'd brought.

'There's one in the dresser drawer.' She turned away and began to busy herself at the stove. There wasn't much to do, just the final touches to the creamed potatoes, and the Vichy carrots and braised celery to be placed in their respective serving dishes, but she was glad of any activity.

It occurred to her that this was the first time she'd entertained a man alone, apart from business meetings, since Jack, and the realisation made her jittery.

The new-look Adam Barnard was another concern.

The clothes he was wearing were clearly expensive, and so was the claret that he was setting to breathe.

She was very conscious that her personal preparations for the evening had been a perfunctory wash and a few strokes of the hairbrush. No make-up or change of clothes for her.

Now that he'd smoothed away the rough edges, she was only too aware of the full force of his attraction. Yet she couldn't afford to be. That was not the purpose of the exercise, she reminded herself vehemently.

She just needed to find out a bit more about him. That was it. That was everything.

As she carried the food to the table she saw that Adam had found some candles during his hunt for the corkscrew and fitted them into the pottery holders which usually stood on the dresser.

'I hope you don't mind,' he said. 'I thought it would add a festive touch.'

In truth, Tara minded quite a lot. Candlelight implied intimacy rather than festivity, she thought restively, but now that the tapers were lit she could hardly make a fuss.

Adam, seemingly unaware of her hesitation, sniffed appreciatively. 'You've gone to a great deal of trouble.'

'Mrs Pritchard did most of it,' she reminded him coolly. She cut into the pie, and served him a lavish wedge.

'Hey—save some for yourself.'

'There's plenty,' she said quickly. 'Actually, I'm not very hungry.'

He looked at her, brows lifted. 'Really?' he drawled. 'We must see what we can do to restore your appetite.'

Cutting out remarks like that would help for a start,

she told him silently. Or was she just being ridiculously twitchy? Looking for trouble where there was none?

Pull yourself together, she ordered herself tersely. Just get through the evening.

In spite of her protest, she found that, once tasted, she couldn't resist the tender chunks of meat and rich gravy under the melting pastry crust. Mrs Pritchard had surpassed herself, she acknowledged gratefully.

The wine was good, too, touching her throat like velvet and filling her mouth with the fragrance of blackcurrant.

As Adam went to refill her glass she swiftly covered it with her hand.

'I'd better not have any more.'

'Why not? You haven't got work tomorrow, and you're not planning to drive anywhere, are you? At least, not tonight.'

She heard that note of laughter in his voice again, and her mouth tightened. He sounded as if he'd been perched inside her head for the last hour or so, observing her mental struggles.

'No,' she said. 'But I know my limitations.'

'That's fine,' he said equably. 'As long as you make sure they don't obscure your potential.'

'My goodness.' She offered him the potatoes. 'Do you write books on self-improvement, by any chance?'

'I don't write books at all.' With equal politeness, he passed her the celery. 'But I apologise if I sounded sententious.'

She flushed. 'No—I didn't mean... That is...'

Aware that she was floundering, she stopped.

'Sometimes a direct question is best,' Adam remarked pensively.

'I don't know what you mean,' Tara said coldly, concentrating on her plate.

'You want to know what I do for a living.' His tone was matter-of-fact. 'Why not just ask?'

'Because that's entirely your own business,' she came back at him, trying to retrieve the situation. 'Nothing to do with me.'

'No,' he said drily. 'But that hasn't stopped you burning up with curiosity from the moment we met. And you have good reason,' he added, after a brief pause. 'Do you spend a lot of time down here on your own?'

'I'm sure Mrs Pritchard has already told you the answer to that,' Tara said, with a snap.

'Is that what's riling you? That I've stolen some kind of march on you?'

'Of course not. Cooking and gossip are her specialities. Everyone knows that.' She put her knife and fork down, colour rising in her face. 'Oh, God, that sounds so bitchy.'

'Just a touch,' he agreed.

She gave him a furious look. 'I'm not usually like it.'

'Then it must be my malign influence,' he said smoothly. 'May I have another piece of pie? You can throw it at me, if you wish.'

She was startled into an unwilling laugh. She pushed the dish towards him. 'Please help yourself.' She paused. 'I haven't made a pudding, but there's cheese and fruit.'

'And all of it for an unwanted guest,' he murmured. 'How incredibly magnanimous. And I'm a draughtsman.'

'Oh,' said Tara, completely taken aback.

He lifted an eyebrow as he transferred meat and pastry to his plate. 'Surprised that I'm so respectable?'

'No,' she denied too swiftly.

'It's a hellish life, but someone has to do it.' He grinned at her. 'Feel reassured?'

No, she thought, but I don't know why.

She said, 'Is that the intention?'

'I think so. For better or worse we're going to be sharing some space.' He leaned across and poured more wine into her glass. 'Let's drink to a better understanding.'

Now, of course, would be the time to tell him she wasn't staying. To come out with some glib excuse for leaving and getting on with her life, well out of harm's way.

But, for some reason she couldn't for the life of her explain, she remained silent.

Adam lifted his glass, and she raised hers obediently in turn.

He looked at her for a long, quiet moment. His blue eyes seemed to glitter in the candlelight, and the table between them was suddenly very narrow.

Tara was staring back at him, as if mesmerised. In those few strange seconds she knew—as if it had already happened—as if he had come to her and drawn her up, out of her chair, into his arms—the touch of his mouth on hers, the brush of his hands on her naked skin. Knew it, and wanted it with a sudden ache of longing too deep for words.

He said softly, 'To us.' And drank.

While Tara sat completely still, her lips slightly parted in shock, and her fingers frozen to the stem of her glass.

CHAPTER THREE

FORTUNATELY, Adam didn't appear to notice her paralysed state, much less guess its cause. He drank the toast, then put down his glass and returned to the remainder of his meal.

Tara, suddenly aware that her hand had started shaking, carefully replaced her own glass on the table too.

She was over-reacting badly, and she knew it. Just as she'd done from the moment she set eyes on him.

It was only a toast, she argued silently. Simply one of those things that people said. It didn't mean anything. It couldn't. And so silly to get het up about something so trivial. So very silly.

But, all the same, she knew that she should never have let herself be talked into sharing her supper with Adam. Wine and candlelight, she thought, her heart hammering. A seriously bad idea. And she needed to bring the evening to an end with despatch.

She clattered the cutlery noisily on to her plate and rose. 'I—I'll get the cheese.'

'Fine.' Adam got to his feet too. 'If you'll show me where everything is, I'll make the coffee.'

It was a perfectly reasonable offer, Tara thought wrathfully as she carried the used dishes to the sink. She could hardly tell him that coffee was off the menu and she was having second thoughts about the cheese, too.

Behave normally, she advised herself. And once you shut the door behind him make sure it stays closed.

There'd been a new pack of coffee among the groceries. She retrieved it from the small larder, then walked over to the dresser and stretched up to the top shelf for the cafetière.

'Allow me.' He was standing right behind her.

'Oh—thank you.' She moved hastily out of the way as Adam reached past her. She was aware, fleetingly, of the faint fragrance of some expensive cologne. He'd not been wearing it earlier when she'd cannoned into him. Then, there'd only been the fresh, clean, quintessentially male scent of his skin, she remembered, suppressing a gasp.

'Is something wrong?'

The last thing she wanted was for him to think she was nervous. That would be putting herself in his power, she reminded herself grimly.

'Not a thing.' She flashed him a meaningless smile, and busied herself arranging cheese, grapes and a few apples on a wooden platter.

'You're like a cat on hot bricks.' Adam set the kettle to boil, then looked past her with a faint grin. 'You should follow her example instead.'

Turning, Tara saw that Melusine had given up her vantage point on the draining board and was now occupying the rocking chair in the corner, her paws tucked neatly under her and her green eyes inscrutable. Buster was stretched out, snoring, on the rug below.

'You see,' Adam went on. 'Initial differences can be settled, and peaceful co-existence achieved.'

'Natures, however, do not basically change,' she said crisply. 'And Melusine and I like our own space.'

'Well, you've got plenty of it here,' he remarked, glancing round him. 'This is a delightful house.' He paused. 'It makes you realise what potential Dean's Mooring could have.'

She stared at him. 'But it's practically derelict,' she said slowly, after a pause. 'It would probably cost—thousands simply to make it habitable.'

'Undoubtedly, but—for the right person—a labour of love.'

'And are you the right person?' She was startled into sharpness. Because this wasn't the plan at all. Dean's Mooring was going to belong to the Lyndon family, thereby ensuring the privacy of Silver Creek.

Oh, Dad, you should have made your move earlier, she reproached her absent parent. Now it could be too late.

'A direct question at last.' Adam spooned coffee into the cafetière, his movements economical and unhurried. As if, somehow, he was right at home in his surroundings, she thought uneasily. 'We're making progress.'

'Yet that,' she said, 'was not a direct answer.'

'The night is young.' He smiled at her, without mockery or calculation, and she felt the warmth of it uncurling insidiously in her deepest self.

The night, she thought grimly, had better start ageing pretty damn quickly.

She found a packet of oatcakes and tipped them on to the platter, then cut a chunk of butter into an earthenware dish.

'This is becoming a feast,' Adam commented as he brought the cafetière to the table. 'Maybe you'll let me cook for you on *Caroline* one evening. Repay the hospitality a little.'

'In that case, you should ask Mrs Pritchard instead,' she returned coolly. 'This was her feast, not mine. I was planning poached eggs on toast.'

His brows lifted. 'Real spinster fare,' he drawled. 'Is that how you see yourself?'

'I don't think my self-image is up for discussion. And this is simply a meal—not a therapy session.' She pushed the platter towards him. 'There's good Cheddar, some Brie, and the blue one's Roquefort.'

'And trespassers will be prosecuted, or worse.' He cut some cheese. He had strong hands, she noticed unwillingly, with long fingers and well-kept nails.

'Talking of trespassing,' she said. 'What exactly brought you to this backwater?'

'I'd always promised myself I'd explore this stretch of river,' he said, after a pause. 'As I had some time off, I decided this was as good a time as any.'

'There isn't a lot to see, and even less to do.'

'That's true,' he said. 'But between a little gentle sketching and taking Buster for long walks I manage to keep busy.' He began, deftly, to peel an apple. 'So, what brings you here?'

Tara shrugged. 'I told you. I like to keep an eye on the house while my parents are away.'

'I hope they appreciate how protective you are.' His eyes glinted at her.

'Indeed they do,' she said. 'And with good reason.'

'I gather they've been using the house for many years.' He cut his apple into quarters. 'They've never thought of selling it?'

Tara gasped. 'Of course not,' she said roundly. 'Why on earth should they?'

Adam gave a faint shrug. 'The right price might be an incentive,' he countered.

'Never in this world.' Tara sat up very straight, her face flushed. 'A lot of family memories are tied up in this house.'

The straight brows drew together. 'Is that necessarily an issue?'

'Naturally it is.'

'Then they must be unique,' he drawled. 'When sentiment and money clash, sentiment usually comes off a poor second.'

'It's nothing to do with sentiment,' Tara said quickly. 'This is their second home—their sanctuary, if you like. When my father worked in the City it was an important means of relaxation for him. We used to come down nearly every weekend to walk and sail. It was Dad's pressure valve. He'd never get rid of it.'

She glared at him. 'So, if you're looking for a cheap weekend retreat, go and look somewhere else,' she added with emphasis.

'You're very keen to see the back of me.' His mouth twisted in amusement. 'If I was the sensitive type, I might get a complex.'

'Oh, not you.' Tara took a bunch of grapes, relishing the cool sweetness against her dry throat. She leaned back in her chair, meeting his gaze squarely. 'You just have to learn that money can't buy everything you see.'

'I'll try to remember that,' he said with suspicious meekness, leaving Tara to pour the coffee with the vexed consciousness that she'd just sounded like a pompous idiot.

She'd allowed this stranger—this intruder—to get under her skin somehow. As if they were playing some game to which he alone knew the rules, she thought uneasily.

She passed him a cup of coffee, offering milk and sugar with a polite murmur. He declined.

'Have you been down here long?' she asked as she sipped the strong, fragrant brew.

'About ten days altogether.'

Her spirits rose slightly. Presumably that indicated holiday, and he'd be back to work and out of her hair after the weekend.

'Have you had good weather?'

'Sunshine and showers. Pretty much what you'd expect for the time of year.' He was grinning again. 'I feel as if I'm being interviewed by a minor royal.'

Tara smacked her cup back into its saucer. 'I thought you preferred direct questions.'

'When they lead to an exchange of information.' The blue eyes challenged her again. 'Not when they're being used as a barrier to hide behind.'

'You have a vivid imagination,' she said coldly. 'What am I supposed to be hiding from, pray?'

'I wish I knew,' he murmured.

'I'm sorry if you don't find me particularly scintillating company,' she went on, as if he hadn't spoken. 'But I've had a very long and rather trying day.'

'With myself as the chief trial, no doubt,' he said cheerfully. He swallowed the rest of his coffee and pushed his chair back. 'So, to prove my heart's in the right place, I'll rid you of my presence as soon as I've helped with the washing up.'

It was pathetic to feel relieved, but she did. She hadn't calculated he would be nearly as easy to shift.

She said, too swiftly, 'There's no need for that. I can manage, thanks,' and saw his mouth twist in wry acknowledgement.

'Then I'll simply thank you for a pleasant evening,' he continued. 'And hope to find you in a more relaxed mood at our next encounter.'

She offered him a tight-lipped smile as she rose too.

'I wouldn't bank on it. I haven't come down here for a rest cure.'

The blue gaze swept her thoughtfully. 'Well, I can hope,' he said. He signalled to Buster, who rose and padded to his side, tail swaying adoringly.

'And then,' he added as he walked to the door, 'you can tell me all about it.'

'All about what?' Tara's brows drew together as she accompanied him out of the kitchen and along the passage to the front door.

He said quite gently, 'About the man who locked you up and threw away the key. That's what. Goodnight, Tara.'

He bent his head, and for one scared, searing moment she thought he was going to kiss her. But even as she stiffened in recoil he took her chin in his hand, turning her face slightly so that all she experienced was the brief, fugitive brush of his lips across her cheek.

Then he opened the door, and, on a rush of cool river air, was gone.

Tara couldn't get to sleep that night. She'd taken her time before retiring. Had washed up and tidied the kitchen while Melusine went for her nightly roam. Had gone round the ground floor rooms making notes about what needed doing until she heard Melusine mewing to be let in again.

If there was any justice, she should have gone out like a light, she thought fretfully as she twisted and turned, and punched her pillow into shape for the umpteenth time.

She tried to tell herself that her sleeplessness was due to the fact that she'd drained the cafetière while she was clearing up, but she knew she was being dishonest.

That it wasn't merely the heavy-duty presence of caffeine in her bloodstream that was bothering her.

There was something far more basic—more fundamental—at fault. Something she didn't want to examine too closely.

If she'd been at the flat, she'd have accepted her insomnia as a temporary hiccup in life's regularity. She'd have got up and got on with something more useful than lying staring into the unforgiving darkness.

Under normal circumstances she'd have done the same here. She could even have made a start on washing down the walls in the dining room, she realised with irritation.

But that would have meant using lights, which would have been clearly visible from the *Caroline*, and, in turn, might have brought Adam Barnard to investigate. To check up on her. And that was the last thing she wanted.

As it was, she'd felt absurdly self-conscious—lighting the lamp in her bedroom, using the bathroom at the side of the house, knowing that he was there, out on the dark water, able to track her movements if he wished. That he could be aware of the exact moment when she climbed into bed and drew the covers over her. She'd never had to deal with this kind of enforced intimacy before, and somehow she didn't know how to cope.

Her skin still seemed to burn where he had kissed her, as if she'd been marked in some way. And yet there was nothing. She knew that because she'd spent a long time in front of the bathroom mirror, staring at her pale face and scared eyes.

Just as she'd spent an even longer while standing at her window, her whole body chilled and tense in her thin cotton nightshirt, as she'd waited and watched through a chink in the curtains for the lights on *Caroline* to go out too.

She was so on edge that she almost cried out when, with a soft chirrup, Melusine landed on the bed, as she did every night. It was comforting to feel the small paws kneading the coverlet in the familiar rhythmic way, and hear the throaty purr.

Oh, Melusine, she thought, stroking the small proud head. If you only knew what a mess I am.

She was still bewildered with herself, at the way she'd behaved with Adam. Once she'd made the decision to have supper with him she should have remained in control throughout, as she'd planned.

Interviewing, after all, was her thing. She should have been able to find some topic of mutual interest on which she could have drawn him out, discovered what made him tick, just as she'd intended. She was good at it. An interested and encouraging listener. Even quite hopeless clients would leave her office probably convinced she'd be their friend for life, and godmother to their children as well.

But this time all the revelations had seemed to be on her side instead. She wasn't sure what she'd given away—or how. But somehow he'd made her stilted—awkward—commonplace. Pushed her on to the defensive.

Where, she realised helplessly, she still remained.

She turned over on her side, staring towards the window, and Melusine, fed up with the constant disturbance, yowled reproachfully and jumped to the floor.

It had been nearly three years since she'd experienced that fatal drag of sensual awareness towards a man. Since she'd even been remotely tempted to acknowledge her body's need. Its sheer physical hunger for human contact. For warmth and affection.

But then, after Jack, it had seemed safer to remain in the wilderness that his departure had created.

'Jack.' She said his name aloud, wrapping her arms round her body, waiting for the shock of pain and humiliation that the evocation of his memory aroused even now.

That was why she tried so hard not to think about him. To relegate him to the back of her mind where he belonged. But tonight, it seemed, he was not to be so easily dismissed.

She'd been twenty-three when they met, heart-whole, with a string of casual relationships behind her, none of which she'd been prompted to translate into any real intimacy.

She had not long joined Marchant Southern, and her career was still at the fledgling stage when, fatefully, she had been invited to a drinks party in the boardroom of her father's company. Gordon Fairclough, one of the other directors, had been celebrating his birthday.

She'd noticed Jack instantly. He'd been with a group of other men, all twenty-somethings, but he'd stood out, tall, dark-haired and swarthy. He'd been talking and laughing, his eyes constantly raking the room, and as he'd seen Tara his gaze had narrowed appraisingly, appreciatively, until she'd turned away in slight confusion.

She'd said to Anna Fairclough, who'd been at school with her, trying to sound casual, 'Who's that? Tall, blue pinstripe, dark red tie.'

Anna peered obligingly through the crowd. 'Oh, some new whizz-kid accountant type, I think.' She pursed her lips. 'Jack—Jack—something. Dad says he's—' She broke off to greet another acquaintance with extravagant delight, and Mr Fairclough's opinion was lost. Tara drifted off to find her parents, and refill her wine glass at the buffet.

She felt a light touch on her arm. 'Actually, it's Jack Halston.' He was smiling down at her. 'Anna's a shocker for names.'

She smiled back, aware she had flushed a little. 'She always was.'

'Do you work for Grainger Associates? I'm still a new boy, but I'm sure I haven't seen you around.'

She said lightly, 'It's a big company. A lot of people work here.'

'Ah,' he said. 'But I'd have noticed you.' He wasn't smiling any more, and the dark gaze was intense, burning into hers. He said quietly, 'You know that, don't you?'

From some far distance she heard herself say, 'Yes.'

In retrospect—and she'd gone over the scene in her mind, time after agonising time—she couldn't have made it more easy for him if she'd tried.

Within a week they were dating. Within the month they were lovers, and she was lost, carried away on a tide of newly discovered passion, gladly surrendering her virginity to him. Consumed by unfamiliar but intoxicating greed.

Jack was experienced and sophisticated, but he seemed delighted by her comparative naivety, and almost amused by her physical innocence.

'You're my own private anachronism, sweet,' he teased her as he coaxed her out of her inhibitions.

She was sharing a flat with two other girls, but when Jack asked her she moved in with him. And for the first time became aware that her parents had reservations.

'But it's so unfair,' she argued heatedly. 'Becky and Harry lived together before they were married. What's so different?'

'Darling, you've only known him a comparatively short time.' Her mother looked worried. 'Are you certain you want to make this kind of commitment quite so soon?'

'I love Jack,' she said. She looked at them both, willing them to understand. To give her their blessing. 'When it's right and good, you just know.'

'What happened to that other boy you were seeing—Mark Roberts?'

'Mark?' Tara echoed in astonishment. 'That was all over months ago. And you weren't keen on him either,' she added accusingly, rounding on her father. 'You said he had no ambition, remember? Well, you can't say that about Jack.'

'I shouldn't dream of it.' Jim Lyndon's tone was mildly ironic. And the look he sent his wife was half-warning, half-resigned.

For the first few months, Tara was in paradise. Marchant Southern only occupied a fraction of her attention. The rest of her creative mind was devoted to making Jack happy. To ensuring the flat was always spotless and tidy, cooking the pasta dishes he loved, keeping his clothes in pristine condition. She was on a learning curve, and her goal was becoming the ideal wife—whenever Jack asked her.

Not that he seemed in any hurry to do so, and this was the only cloud on her horizon. She wanted to wear his ring—to have his baby. It was the next logical step towards the perfect happiness she saw as her right.

I'm so lucky, she would tell herself each day, listening to girlfriends and colleagues telling unhappy stories about tiffs, rifts, and the unending search for Mr Right. Jack and I were made for each other.

Once, she tried to tell Anna how she felt, but her friend's response was muted, and the subject rapidly changed.

Poor Anna, Tara thought. Judging by her remarks about being too trusting, she's going through a rocky patch with Gavin. It was tactless of me to advertise my own happiness like that.

It was at a housewarming party thrown by some newly married friends when she first realised that Jack might have other ideas about the future of their relationship.

The house was only half furnished. They sat on packing cases, drank supermarket plonk out of paper cups, ate vegetable curry from plates that didn't match, and laughed a lot.

Later, lying in bed, watching him undress with the usual slow curl of anticipation deep within her, she said, 'That was fun, wasn't it?'

Jack shrugged. 'I thought it was a shambles. I can't believe they'd actually invite people round with the place in that state.'

Tara propped herself on an elbow. 'You don't mean that.'

'I'm perfectly serious.' He looked at her in the mirror, his eyes steady and rather hard. 'The house may be all right one day—if Fiona doesn't start dropping babies and they can afford to do it up properly. But they've got married on a shoestring, and that's ridiculous.'

'But they love each other,' she protested, feeling a sudden chill.

'Naturally, my sweet dope, or they wouldn't be married at all. But Colin still has a way to go in his job, and they'd have done better to postpone.'

Is that how you feel? She wanted to ask him, but the words somehow wouldn't come. Because, she realised, she wasn't sure she wanted to hear his answer.

Then he came to bed, and her doubts were swept aside in their lovemaking.

And when, some six weeks later, he told her he was taking her out for a special dinner because he had something to ask her, she decided, fizzing with suppressed excitement, that he'd clearly had a change of heart.

It was a wonderful meal, but Jack seemed edgy. Or perhaps he was just nervous, she thought tenderly. But why? Surely he knew what her answer would be?

When they reached the coffee stage, and he'd still said nothing, Tara nerved herself.

'You...you said you had something to ask me,' she prompted him, smiling.

He nodded rather jerkily. 'As a matter of fact, yes. You see, darling, there's a whisper that Cadham, our head of department, is taking early retirement.' He laughed. 'Frankly he'll be no great loss. His ideas are rooted in the Dark Ages. Everyone's saying our whole section needs someone young and vigorous to pick it up and shake it into the Millennium.'

There was no need to stir her coffee but she did so, watching it swirl round the spoon. Aware of a sudden odd tension within her.

She said quietly, 'And do you have someone in mind for the job?'

Jack laughed again. 'Of course, my sweet. I'm hoping they'll offer it to me.'

'To you?' She couldn't keep the note of incredulity out of her voice, and he looked annoyed.

'OK, I know I'm not tops in order of seniority, but what does that matter? I can do the job. And I seriously want it.'

She shrugged, avoiding his gaze. 'Then if Peter Cadham does retire, you'd better apply for it. I hope you won't be too disappointed if things don't go your way.'

'Ah, but I intend they shall,' Jack said softly. He stretched a hand across the table and took hers. 'And you, my love, can help.'

'You think they'll come to Marchant Southern for candidates?' She was bewildered. 'They never have in the past. And if they did I wouldn't be dealing with it. I'm too junior myself.'

She saw his mouth tighten, and realised he hadn't relished the word 'junior'.

'To hell with Marchant Southern,' he said impatiently. 'I'm talking about your father. You know as well as I do that he'll have a big say in the appointment.' His tone softened, became appealing. 'I thought you could use your powers to persuade him to speak up for me.'

So that was what the intimate dinner had been leading up to. She felt sick with disappointment, and suddenly afraid.

She said, stammering a little, 'But I couldn't. And why should he listen to me anyway?'

'Because you're supposed to have some expertise in recruitment, for one thing,' he said. 'And you're Daddy's little girl, for another. And he'll want you to be happy.'

His fingers tightened round hers, almost hurting her.

'Think about it, love. You want to get married, don't you? Well, look on this as a stepping stone—a short cut. We'd have to wait years on my present salary. If I got Cadham's job we could have everything we wanted, without scrimping and scraping.'

He smiled at her coaxingly. 'I want to spoil you—treat you as you deserve. Give you a proper setting. And if I was his son-in-law your father could be sure of my total company loyalty, as well,' he added insinuatingly.

She said huskily, 'Jack—I'd be just as happy to start in a small way. We could get married and go on living in the flat. You'll get a promotion eventually—I know it. Maybe something better will come along—with another company.'

'Sweetheart.' He was still smiling, but there was an undercurrent of irritation now. 'I don't want to move. My sights are set. I don't know why you're making all this fuss. I thought you'd be pleased. That you'd be glad to do this little thing for me.'

She looked down at the table. She said quietly, 'I don't think I know quite how I feel. But I'll speak to my father, if that's really what you want. Although I can't guarantee a thing,' she added. 'You must understand that.'

'Oh, for God's sake, Tara. Your old man's always given you and your sister anything you've ever wanted. Everyone knows that.'

Tara crumpled her napkin into a ball. 'Then everyone knows more than I do,' she said stonily. 'And now I'd like to go home, please.'

The next ten days were a nightmare, with constant pressure from Jack colliding headlong with her own reluctance.

Eventually, wearily, and wanting to avoid their first real quarrel at all costs, Tara agreed to phone her parents and suggest she join them at Silver Creek for the weekend.

Jack, she knew, would not accompany her. He'd been down once, just for the day, in those first ecstatic weeks, but he'd seemed ill at ease in his surroundings.

Afterwards, Tara could see why. He'd expected to find a millionaire's weekend retreat—a mansion with sculpted lawns sweeping down to the water, probably with its own tennis court and a swimming pool. Instead he'd found a shabby family home with only one bathroom, and an elderly sailing dinghy.

She was on edge all weekend, wondering how to bring the subject up. In the end her father did it for her, mentioning casually over a game of Scrabble that they were drawing up a short-list for Peter Cadham's job.

'You'll miss him,' Barbara said, frowning over her tiles.

'God, yes. He's been like a rock. But young Ritchie has been working closely with him for the past year, and he's the most likely candidate.'

Later, when her mother had gone up to bed, Tara said, 'Dad, is it definite about Ian Ritchie? Has he been offered the department?'

Jim Lyndon was fixing the guard in front of the fire. 'No, not yet. Why do you ask?' His voice was quizzical. 'Do you know of a better candidate?'

She swallowed. 'I thought—Jack.'

'Did you, my dear—or was the thought really his?' He waited for a moment, his shrewd gaze fixed on her flushed, unhappy face, then sighed. 'But I'm afraid I must disappoint you. Jack has yet to convince me and the rest of the board that he has the makings of a top manager. In the short term he hasn't nearly enough experience, and is inclined to cut corners and take unnecessary risks as a consequence.'

She bit her lip. 'I know you've never liked him...'

'That's not quite true. At the moment I'm trying very hard not to dislike him.' He paused. 'But I know how much it must have cost you to approach me like this, so I won't be angry with you.'

He got up, dusting his hands. 'However, I'll say this before we drop the subject. Jack is still young, and it's early days both in the company and your relationship. He has plenty of time to prove himself.'

She said fiercely, 'And he will.' She hesitated. 'Dad—wouldn't it be possible for him to be shortlisted—given an interview? It would encourage him so much.'

'Oh, does he need encouragement?' Mr Lyndon asked mildly. He gave a slight shrug. 'It seems a pretty pointless exercise to me, but if it will make things easier for you I suppose I've no real objection.'

Jack was jubilant when he received the internal memo telling him he'd indeed been short-listed. He brought home a bottle of champagne and an extravagant bunch of red roses, which Tara accepted wanly, feeling like Judas.

He was so confident, she thought anxiously. So sure. She wished now that she hadn't asked...

And afterwards, when Ian Ritchie's appointment was announced, Jack seemed stunned, stonily incredulous. But when she went to him, tried to put her arms round him to comfort him, he turned from her almost menacingly, his face a harsh stranger's.

He curtly rejected the meal she'd cooked and went out, for the first time not asking her to go with him.

And it was the small hours when he returned, sliding into bed beside her without noticing, apparently, that she'd been lying awake, waiting for him and worrying.

She told herself it was just disappointment. That he'd feel different—more optimistic—the following day. And then maybe she'd stop feeling that she was standing on the edge of some precipice—where all it would take would be one breath of wind to carry her over the brink and down to destruction.

But I was wrong, Tara thought now, staring into the darkness. Because the precipice was real, and it was there—waiting for me.

CHAPTER FOUR

SHE didn't want to do this, she thought. She didn't want to remember. But the images were there, burning in her brain. Everything Jack had said. Everything he'd done.

For three years she'd fought to keep them at bay. Now the cupboard was open, and the skeletons were crowding upon her.

Nothing had ever been the same again after Jack failed to get the job, although she had done her best to persuade herself otherwise.

She'd tried to talk to him about it. 'Jack—I did try—really.'

The dark eyes were bottomless wells of indifference. 'Not hard enough, obviously.'

He hardly spent any time in the flat. He was out nearly every evening, and when he joined her in bed he reeked of cigarettes and alcohol. Sometimes she even thought she detected the hint of a woman's scent on his skin. Opium, she thought. Something she never used. And then silently berated herself for being paranoid.

What she could not pretend was that Jack still wanted her sexually. Whereas once he'd been unable to keep his hands off her, now he seemed to be doing his best to avoid all physical contact with her. And when, bewildered and unhappy, she tried to make a few shy overtures of her own, he turned on her almost brutally.

'For God's sake, Tara, I'm under enough stress right

now without you hassling me for sex. Give it a rest, will you?'

If he'd struck her in the face she could not have been more shocked. She never tried again.

And self-censure wasn't all she had to bear. Her immediate boss, Leo Southern, called her into his office and gave her a stinging dressing-down over her recent attitude to her work. 'Sloppy' was one word he used. And 'ineffectual'.

'When you joined us, Tara, you were keen—you were hot.' He threw himself back in his chair and surveyed her, his mouth compressed. 'Now half the time you don't seem to be on the same planet. You'd better pull yourself together, and damned quickly.'

He saw the panicked look in her eyes, and his tone softened marginally. 'Listen, take the rest of the day off. Do that exercise we sometimes give new clients. List your goals, and the positive and negative factors that affect them. Then work out how to eliminate the negative, however painful. I'll see you tomorrow.'

She didn't argue. She knew she was being given one last chance, and that she'd already blotted her copybook by bringing her private life into office hours.

As she travelled back on the underground she knew she had to get things sorted out with Jack. Her job was precious to her. She couldn't afford to jeopardise it. And she couldn't lose Jack either. She had to fight for both of them.

She would begin by telling him how much she loved him, she thought. Offer to do anything that would change their life back to the way it had been. After all, there was no place for pride in love.

And Jack's pride had been hurt too, she realised sombrely. Perhaps he thought she wouldn't want him any more, now that he'd failed. She needed to show him how wrong he was. How much faith she had in him.

We should get married, she thought. Face the world united. I can talk him round. I must.

As she approached the apartment block she glanced up, and saw with shock that one of their windows was slightly open.

How did that happen? she wondered, quickening her step. Which of us was the last to leave this morning? It must have been me, yet I'm sure I checked the windows. I always do.

She went up the stairs to their floor, two at a time. As she fitted her key into one of the safety locks she tensed, because it wasn't fastened. In fact the whole door was on the latch, she realised, pushing it open and wondering sickly what scene of devastation she was going to find.

But the living room looked just the same as usual. Or did it? She looked around slowly, registering Jack's overcoat lying across the sofa, a bottle of wine half-drunk on the coffee table. A pair of high-heeled shoes abandoned carelessly underneath it. Not hers.

There was the sound of a door opening, and she turned to see Jack emerging from the bedroom. Their bedroom. He was wearing his red silk dressing gown, the sash loosely knotted round his waist, and beneath it he was naked. He had a cigarette in one hand, and in the other he was carrying two empty wine glasses by their stems.

When he saw Tara, he checked, his brows lifting sharply.

'Well, well,' he said softly. 'What a charming surprise. And so opportune. At least I don't have to do your packing for you.'

Her throat felt parched suddenly. It was difficult to articulate the words. 'Packing? I—I don't understand what you mean.'

'Yes, you do, darling.' He was smiling at her. 'I'm revoking your temporary tenancy here. Giving you notice to quit. And the sooner the better.'

'Quit?' She stared at him. 'You—want me to—leave?'

Jack sighed with exaggerated patience. 'And you're supposed to be such a bright girl,' he said mockingly.

'But you can't—I can't...' She swallowed. 'This is some awful joke. It must be.'

'No joke.' He shrugged. 'Just a game that I've become bored with. But I was prepared to go on playing while there was a chance you might push me up the corporate ladder. But I now know that's not going to happen, so I've found a new playmate. And you, my sweet, are surplus to requirements—in bed and out of it.'

She said hoarsely, 'You don't mean this. You *can't.* Jack, don't say such things. I love you. We love each other.'

'Correction,' he said. 'I loved the fact that you were the boss's daughter, and that you could be useful to me. But you blew it.' He smiled at her, and for the first time she saw the cruelty beneath the facile charm.

'We were going to be married.' The words were wrung from her.

'So we were,' he agreed. 'I'd have even made that sacrifice for a seat on the board. But to tell you the truth I'm rather glad your father cancelled my entry. It was going to be a hell of an act to sustain. You're terribly earnest, you know, darling, and a bit of a drag sexually. Oh, you were a novelty at first, but that soon wore off. And no amount of girlish enthusiasm is ever going to equal natural-born talent.'

The pain had been there from the moment she saw him walk out of the bedroom and realised what was happening, but she'd managed to hold it back. Now, she felt its teeth snap into her, taking hold and tearing at her, flesh and spirit.

Yet somehow she managed to lift her head. 'In that case, I'd better get my things.'

'Exactly.' He poured some more wine into the glasses. 'You realise, of course, I have a guest.'

'Yes,' she said. 'I'm sorry to have intruded.'

'As a matter of interest, why are you here?' He drank some wine, watching her. 'You haven't got the sack, too, I hope.' He saw the shock on her face, and laughed. 'Oh, yes, I was "let go" last week. Some kind of rationalisation programme, I gather, which only involved me. They offered me salary in lieu of notice, plus a sweetener, and I took it. A mate of mine is running some mining company out in Brazil, and I'm going to join him, just in case you were concerned about me,' he added.

'I'm not,' she said. 'My sympathies are with Brazil. The rainforest has enough problems already.'

'A kitten showing her claws?' he asked unpleasantly. 'Don't try and play rough with me, darling, or you'll get hurt.'

She was hurt already. She was disintegrating, bleeding to death. How could he not see that?

'I'll ask Julie to wait in the bathroom while you clear out,' he went on. 'I'd be grateful if you'd hurry. She's forgotten more about sex than you'll ever know, and I'm keen to jog her memory again.'

She tried not to look at the rumpled bed as she emptied drawers into her cases, piling the clothes and possessions on top of each other without regard. The scent of Opium hung heavy in the air, and she knew she would hate its fragrance until her dying day. She left her keys on the coffee table and went out, closing the door quietly behind her.

She hailed a passing taxi, and told it to take her to her parents' house in Chelsea.

The driver glanced at her in his mirror. 'You all right, gal?'

'Yes,' she said, tears chasing themselves down her white face. 'Never better.'

Tara sat bolt upright in bed. She was shaking and her cotton shirt was clinging to her damp body, as if she'd been startled into wakefulness from some dreadful nightmare.

She pushed back the covers, and, stumbling slightly, went over to the window, drawing back the curtains. The sky was silver with daylight, and there was a faint mist rising from the river. Riding silently at anchor, *Caroline* looked like a ghost ship, but she was there, and only too real, Tara thought broodingly.

She sat down, resting her folded arms on the window-sill.

She knew exactly why the past had come back to haunt her. The reason was sleeping in his cabin, a stone's throw away, out on the water.

Adam Barnard had imposed himself on her life—impinged upon her consciousness in a way that no man had been permitted to do since Jack.

Never again. That was what she'd kept telling herself in the stunned, heartbroken weeks that had followed their break-up. No man is ever getting that close to me again.

Every ugly word he'd spoken had seemed to crawl like acid over her skin. She had hardly been able to bear to look at herself in the mirror. Drab, she'd thought, boring, undesirable. She would carry them, stamped on her, like the brand of Cain her whole life through.

She had not simply fallen for Jack. She had trusted him, believed in him, so his betrayal had been total.

When he had gone, the truth slowly began to emerge. People who had kept silent in view of her obvious happiness had come shamefacedly forward, Anna among them.

'Babe, I did warn you—at my father's birthday party. Dad said he was a bad lot from the first. All flash and no substance.'

Tara hadn't argued with her. After all, she'd thought wearily, even if Anna *had* completed her warning, would she have believed her?

Julie had not been Jack's first act of infidelity by any means, and he'd jeered openly at Tara's gullibility for believing him when he'd said he was working late, or attending weekend seminars.

'You know I hate to leave you, sweet, but it's for our future,' he'd used to whisper to her ardently, and the memory left her shaking and nauseated.

Her parents had been wonderful, her mother openly distressed when Tara had insisted on going back to work the day after she'd arrived at the Chelsea house in a state near collapse.

'I need to work,' Tara had told her bluntly. 'That way I don't have to think.'

Coldly, single-mindedly, she'd thrown herself into

her career. Within a year she'd gained promotion, and an appropriate pay rise. She'd found her flat, decorated it, and furnished it slowly and with care. Finally she'd acquired Melusine.

A career—a life—a companion. Who could ask for anything more?

She'd believed she was totally self-sufficient—'fire-proof' even—and now here she was, dizzy with lust over the first attractive man to cross her path, she derided herself.

Except, of course, that wasn't strictly true. Not by any means. She'd met men every day of her life over the past years, who were more charming, more glamorous than Adam Barnard would ever be.

And, quite apart from Becky's well-meaning efforts, she'd had plenty of opportunities to embark on new relationships. But she'd always steered clear, retreating behind her barrier of cool reserve when someone threatened to come close.

It wasn't difficult. She only had to recall the devastation that Jack had left behind him.

She was afraid of being hurt again. Of being used. Of being savaged and abandoned.

And, most of all, of being found out. Of being exposed all over again as dull—unlovable—undesirable.

Because love—or what passed for it—hurt. That was what she needed to remember. All she needed to remember. She could never again allow herself to become the broken thing of three years ago.

She'd worked hard to gain control of her life—of herself—and she wasn't going to jeopardise that for a passing attraction, however potent.

She'd created her own safety net—a private hedge

of thorns around herself. And if Adam Barnard knew what was good for him he'd stay on his own side of it.

Not that she'd given him a chance to do otherwise. Now that she'd recognised the potential danger he could pose, she would deal with it.

And eventually he would grow tired of the cool, unchanging civility. The lack of response, unsmiling, even uncomprehending, to his advances.

And, like the others, he would move on. Find some other warmer, more willing lady. Leave her in peace.

Only this time peace might not be so easy to come by, a sly voice whispered in her head.

Sighing, she got to her feet and went downstairs, with Melusine weaving round her legs. She poured the cat some milk, then filled the kettle and set it to boil. She took a carton of orange juice from the fridge and drank a glassful, gasping at its cold tartness against her throat.

While she was waiting for the kettle she went back up to the bathroom and began running water into the tub, adding a capful of fragrant oil, filling the room with the dusky scent of geraniums. Her disturbed night had left her with vague aches and pains, and a strange restlessness which she wanted to soak away.

She made herself a strong mug of coffee and sipped it while she lay submerged, letting the hot, scented water work its magic on her.

Everything's going to be all right, she assured herself, stretching luxuriously. There may have been a few underground tremors, but the citadel still stands. And that's how it will stay.

She finished her coffee and lifted herself from the tub, swathing herself in a towel.

She was humming to herself as she re-entered her

bedroom, chose underwear and a T-shirt and cotton trousers for the day ahead. The early overcast sky was clearing and the sun was coming through. It was going to be a hot day if she was any judge.

She paused, her attention caught by a movement outside. She went to the window and stood for a moment, watching the river. A moorhen had emerged from the reeds and was swimming sedately, her brood a brown ripple in her wake, but that wasn't what she had seen. Or she didn't think so.

And then she saw him, across the river, walking on the opposite bank among the clustering silver birches which sparkled in the early sunlight.

A dark figure, tall and purposeful, the dog frisking round him.

Another early riser, she thought. Or perhaps he couldn't sleep either. She felt a tingle of something like pleasure curl along her nerve-endings. Felt her throat tighten.

As she watched, he stopped suddenly and turned towards the house, as if aware of her scrutiny. As if across the gleaming water their eyes had met and locked, holding them in thrall to each other.

But that's nonsense, Tara thought, feeling her breathing quicken. He can't see me. The sun will be in his eyes. It's impossible. I *know*...

Common sense told her to get away from the window anyway, but she remained where she was, her eyes fixed on the dark, motionless figure. Her hands seemed to move of their own volition, without any conscious impulse on her part, loosening the damp towel and tossing it away from her on to the bed. Leaving her naked in the sun's dazzle.

She lifted her arms, stroking the heavy fall of her

hair back from her face with a sigh, then let her hands slip down, touching herself slowly, exploringly. Cupping her breasts, measuring the span of her slender waist, outlining the curves of hips and flanks as if she was displaying herself. Making an invisible offering of her entire being to the silent watcher in the trees.

But he could not see, and would never know, therefore she was safe. She felt a smile as old as the earth touch and lift the corners of her mouth. Felt her nipples harden in exquisite excitement, and the core of her turn to sweet, liquid warmth.

In that moment she seemed to know him—the touch of his hands—the drugging warmth of his mouth—the brush of his skin against hers—the silken thrust of his possession. All of him.

She sighed, and, closing her eyes, she stretched, a long languorous movement that arched her whole body. And when she looked again he had gone. There was only the sun, the trees, and the ripple of the water.

Perhaps she'd only imagined him. Had created his presence out of her own need.

And stopped right there, her hand stealing to her mouth in shock and repudiation.

My God, she thought, what am I thinking?

Was she going completely crazy—out of her head? Standing in front of the window with nothing on, having erotic daydreams about—a passing stranger.

It is time, she told herself grimly, that you got on with your life.

Tara put the cans of gloss and emulsion paint in the boot of her car, and tucked the box with the filler, the sandpaper and new brushes in beside them.

'That'll keep you out of mischief,' the shopkeeper had commented as she'd paid the bill.

And that, she'd thought, was exactly the idea. She'd given him a non-committal smile and a word of thanks.

She needed something to occupy her time and engage her attention. Something that would stop her brooding over stupid and dangerous fantasies by day, and send her to bed at night too weary to dream.

She closed the boot, and stood for a moment looking down the street. It wasn't a large place—little more than a village, really—but it had all the amenities, including an estate agency.

While I'm here, she thought, I'll pop in and see what's being asked for Dean's Mooring. I should think the price is rock-bottom by now. And, if so, I could probably afford to buy it myself. Make it my spare time project. Do it up slowly, and just the way I want it.

The estate agency was empty when she went in, except for a middle-aged man busy at a filing cabinet. He turned and gave her a friendly smile.

'May I help you?'

'I hope so. There's a property at Silver Creek I'm interested in—Dean's Mooring. I think you're selling it?'

He looked at her with genuine surprise. 'I'm afraid not. As far as I know that particular property is not on the market with anyone.'

'Oh.' Tara digested that, frowning. 'What's the hold-up, I wonder. Something to do with probate, perhaps?'

'I couldn't say.' He paused. 'I believe Mr Hanman of Hanman and Brough in Middle Street is handling the estate. You could always ask him—after the holiday, of course.'

Tara sighed. 'I was hoping to get things moving right away.'

'We have other houses on our books, if you're looking for a riverside frontage,' he said hopefully. 'I'd be happy to show them to you.'

Tara shook her head, smiling. 'I'm afraid I'm only interested in Dean's Mooring. But thanks anyway.'

She would just have to be patient until the Bank Holiday was over.

First thing on Tuesday morning, I'll come in and see Mr Hanman, she thought. Find out what the delay is.

It was aggravating, but at least she'd taken the first step, she consoled herself as she drove home.

Back at the house, she put on one of her father's old shirts as an overall, tied her hair up in a scarf, and threw herself determinedly into her preparations. She'd already decided to begin with the dining room, and tugged the furniture into the centre of the room, covering it with dust sheets.

She deliberately kept away from the front of the house, not wanting to catch any untoward glimpses of *Caroline* or her master, but when it was time to take down the curtains she found she had little choice.

Because Adam was right there, facing the house, sitting at an easel which he'd set up near the jetty, apparently absorbed in painting.

'Bloody nerve,' Tara muttered under her breath, jerking the inoffensive curtains free from their rings with more force than the task required.

And yet there was no reason for her to be het up. Plenty of other painters had used Silver Creek House and its environs as their subject before this, and there'd been no objections from her or anyone else in the family. Indeed, her mother was prone to taking them cups of coffee, sandwiches, and homemade lemonade on hot days.

But pigs would fly before she offered Adam Barnard as much as the crumbs from the bread bin, she vowed as she descended from her steps, the curtains draped over her arm.

She worked feverishly, cleaning the paintwork with sugar soap, filling and smoothing, until a plaintive protest from Melusine alerted her to the fact it was already midday.

She fed Melusine, then heated herself a can of chicken soup, pouring it into a mug and sipping it, perched on the shrouded dining-room table while she contemplated the next stage of her labours. She'd chosen a creamy primrose emulsion for the walls, and she was itching to get started, knowing it would take two coats to cover the rather dingy blue presently in place.

When the knock sounded at the front door she stiffened, her mouth tightening. No prizes for guessing who that was, she thought. Sitting where he was, he couldn't have missed all the activity inside the house. Indeed, when she'd been rubbing down part of the window-frame he'd even waved to her. And now curiosity had brought him over.

She drank the last of her soup, put down the mug, and went reluctantly to answer the door. At the last moment she switched her scowl for a look of haughty enquiry, and was glad when she threw the door open and discovered it wasn't Adam at all, but a complete stranger. A stocky man with a moustache and a crumpled grey suit.

'Good afternoon, madam.' His smile seemed to have too many teeth. 'We're visiting homes in the neighbourhood, offering spot cash for antiques and collectables. I'd be happy to give you a free valuation on any item.'

'No, thank you,' said Tara, and went to close the door, only to find his foot was in it.

'Why don't you have a little look round, madam?' he urged. 'You'd be surprised how many unwanted items you could have tucked away, just waiting to make money for you.'

'There's nothing,' Tara said coldly. His insistence was irritating, she thought, noting over his shoulder that Adam and his easel had vanished.

'I could always have a look-see for myself.' He'd taken a step forward and was blocking the doorway. 'Even if it's just to update your contents valuation for insurance. You'd be surprised how many people are under-insured and have reason to be grateful to me. Or maybe I could have a word with your husband?' he added insinuatingly.

He'd taken another step forward, forcing Tara to fall back, and now he was actually in the hall. His neck bulged over his collar, and under the cheap suit his shoulders looked uncomfortably wide.

She lifted her chin. 'No, you can't,' she said curtly, knowing that he was well aware she was alone. 'And I'd like you to go. Now.'

He chuckled. 'How many times have I heard that before, I wonder? And it invariably leads to me doing some nice, friendly business.' He paused. 'Now, why don't you give me the guided tour, like a good girl? And I'll give you a fair price for anything that takes my eye.'

She realised that she was frightened, but that it was important not to let him see it if she was to have any hope of getting him outside the house again. The air seemed charged with a mixture of pungent aftershave and sweat that made her stomach churn. If one of those pink, moist hands touched her, she knew she would be sick.

At first she didn't realise what the low rumbling sound was, because her ears were half deafened by her own pulse-beats. Then she realised it was a dog's soft, threatening growl, and saw, just behind the intruder, Buster with his hackles up and his lips drawn back from his teeth, his whole attitude pure menace. And beyond him, she saw with a swift surge of relief, Adam, with his hands in his pockets, his casual stance contradicted by the icy watchfulness in the blue eyes.

He said quietly, 'Is there a problem, darling? I was just on the boat. You should have called me.'

The newcomer turned sharply, giving Buster an unfriendly look. 'Is that dog safe?'

'Usually,' Adam said pleasantly. 'Except, of course, when he feels he has to defend my wife. And as he seems to dislike you, I suggest you do as she asks, and leave.'

'No need for that,' the other blustered defensively, as he edged past Buster. 'I just came to see if I could do some business.'

'No sale,' Adam said. 'And I've taken the number of your van. If you make any attempt to return, I shall inform the police.'

With a muttered obscenity, the dealer squeezed out of the hall and disappeared rapidly round the corner of the house. A moment later, they heard the sound of an engine being hastily revved, before the vehicle was driven off at speed.

The enemy disposed of, Buster sat, flattened his ears, and offered Tara a beguiling paw.

'Thank you,' she said, accepting the paw and smoothing the dog's head awkwardly with her other hand. She did not look directly at Adam. 'How did you know?'

'I'd taken Buster for a run across the fields, and saw the van parked at the end of the lane. Then I heard you both talking and thought I'd better intervene.'

'I'm—grateful.' She paused, gathering her resources. 'But there was really no need. I—I could have managed.'

'Could you?' he said softly. 'Now you looked to me like a lady on the run.'

'But appearances are often deceptive.' This time she did look at him, to find him leaning against the door-post, all polite attention, apart from the cynical grin twisting his mouth.

She raised her voice a notch. 'I assure you the situation was under control.'

'So, if he'd grabbed you, you'd have been able to get away, no danger?'

Her hesitation was fractional. 'Of course.'

'Then show me.' He took one stride and reached for her, jerking her off balance into his arms and holding her there imprisoned and helpless against the lean, hard length of his body.

Tara clenched her fists, pushing unavailingly at his chest. 'Let me go, damn you...'

'I hope that's not your only line of defence,' he said mockingly. Still holding her effortlessly, he captured her wrists in one hand and lifted them over her head. 'Because it doesn't work. What are you going to do now?'

She kicked him hard, but, although he winced

slightly, the soft canvas shoes she was wearing did little damage, and he still retained his grip.

'Be careful,' he warned softly. 'You could break a toe like that.'

'I'd like to break your neck,' she threw at him, her face flushed and furious. She felt ridiculous, and, what was worse, vulnerable.

Because she knew, without room for doubt, that she was the one who could end up broken—shattered into little tiny pieces.

'I'm sure you would.' He was watching her with close appraisal, as if his eyes were searching for something in the depths of hers. 'But use it as a learning experience,' he went on. 'Don't start confrontations you can't win.'

Tara bit her lip, hard.

'Will you let go of me, please?' She tried to hide the urgency in the appeal. She was altogether too conscious of his proximity—of the warmth of his body penetrating her layers of clothing, seeping into bone, tissue and blood, and turning them to fire.

Her breasts were crushed against the wall of his chest. His breathing had roughened, and she could feel it fanning the tendrils of hair that had escaped from her scarf.

When he slowly lowered his head she could almost taste his mouth on hers, and her eyes closed as she waited, breathlessly.

Only to feel the clasp on her wrists slacken suddenly. To find herself free—completely disengaged. All contact broken. All the small flames dying.

Her eyes flew open. He was in the doorway, a black silhouette against the brightness of the day.

'If you're wondering why I haven't taken advantage

of the situation,' he said, his voice reaching her from some infinity of distance, 'I should, maybe, make something clear.'

He paused, as if weighing his words. Even so, Tara wasn't prepared for what came next.

'It so happens that I'm going to be married quite soon,' he went on. 'So any kind of casual relationship is right off the cards. And I don't think it's what either of us would want, anyway—even if circumstances were different. Am I right?'

'Yes.' She was proud of the cool, crisp way that she snapped back at him.

She saw him nod. 'We seem to have found common ground at last.' He paused again. 'You've just had a nasty experience, and, no matter how well you were dealing with it, I felt you needed a friend. I still think so, and I'm prepared to be here for you if you want— and *only* if you want. Think it over.'

And, snapping his fingers to the dog, he walked away.

CHAPTER FIVE

THERE was something definitely therapeutic about painting, Tara decided as she vigorously rollered the primrose emulsion across the wall. It was symbolic too—an erasing of past mistakes. The presentation of a fresh and shining face to the world.

And, talking of mistakes, she thought grimly, she was well aware she'd been on the verge of making a monster one. The kind of ghastly, irretrievable slip that could have haunted her worst nightmares for years to come.

And Adam Barnard of all people had been the one to point out the error of her ways. Now there was an irony, she mused without pleasure as she tuned her tiny portable radio to a classical music channel. He'd stopped her in her tracks, and started her thinking clearly and sanely again.

And she should be grateful to him. So where was the surge of heartfelt relief?

Instead, she'd simply closed the door on his departing figure and said, 'So, that's that.'

But her voice, even to her own ears, had sounded oddly flat, and she hadn't turned any cartwheels on her way back to the dining room either.

Yet the news that Adam was committed to a relationship should not have caused her a moment's surprise. He was attractive, apparently solvent, and clearly at an age where settling down had become a feasible option. End of story.

In spite of herself, she could not resist speculating about his fiancée.

Dark and sultry, she wondered, or the bubbly girl-next-door type? One certainty was that she'd harbour a deep well-spring of passion to match his own. Instinct told her that he would tolerate nothing less, and the knowledge made her skin warm suddenly, and her mouth go dry.

She stood, staring into space, her mind spinning images of Adam, naked and powerful in the act of possession, his face taut, his eyes hungry as he stared down at the woman of his desire.

A little sensual shiver curled between her shoulder-blades and was gone, leaving her with an odd feeling of emptiness. Of bleakness.

She moved suddenly, swiftly, shaking off her reverie with an impatient toss of her head. Jolting herself back to reality.

Where, she discovered crossly, she'd been allowing paint to drip on to the floorboards. Muttering, she mopped up the splashes with a damp cloth, then attacked the wall with her roller again.

She should concentrate on the job in hand, she told herself fiercely, instead of troubling her head over a girl she would never meet.

Melusine, who'd been snoozing in a patch of sunlight on the dust-sheeted table, uncoiled herself and jumped lightly to the ground, tail held high as she stalked to the door and waited for her mistress to come and open it for her.

'You choose your moments,' Tara told her severely, replacing her roller in its tray and following her. As she opened the door she was immediately aware of movement—alien sounds in the hall beyond that her radio had drowned.

Oh, God, she thought her whole body tensing. She wanted to grab Melusine back to safety, but it was too late. The cat was swaying in full seductive mode towards the front door, uttering a chirrup of pleasure as she butted her head against the legs of the intruder.

Tara's apprehensive peep round the door changed into a full-blooded glare as she realised exactly who was standing at the front door, busy with a screwdriver, while Buster sat meekly beside him, looking as if butter wouldn't melt in his mouth.

'You,' she yelped. 'What the hell do you think you're doing?'

'Hello,' Adam said. 'I hope I didn't startle you. I did knock, but I was no match for Brahms.' He nodded at the doorframe. 'I'm fixing a chain for you, to keep visitors like your dealer friend at bay.'

'A chain?' she repeated. 'Where did that come from?'

'The other house,' Adam said.

Words almost failed her. 'You mean you stole it from Dean's Mooring?' she managed at last.

His brows drew together consideringly. 'I prefer "liberated."'

'Whatever,' Tara said grimly. 'The fact remains you broke in...'

'I didn't have to,' he said. 'The back door was unlocked.'

Oh, indeed, Tara thought, bristling. Then it had no right to be. And that was another matter she'd be raising when she saw Mr Hanman on Tuesday. The security of Dean's Mooring was his responsibility, after all.

'But that doesn't mean you can simply walk in and

help yourself to any piece of convenient hardware,' she objected. 'I can't believe you've really done this.'

'Dean's Mooring is empty and semi-derelict.' He made it sound matter-of-fact, and perfectly reasonable. 'On the face of it, your need for the chain seemed rather more urgent.' He smiled at her. 'And you can always replace it in due course—if you feel that strongly.'

'Thank you,' she said. 'I shall do exactly that.' She paused. 'Tell me, have you always had this cavalier attitude to other people's property?'

'No,' he said promptly. 'I've always been a solid citizen without a stain on my law-abiding character. It must be your pernicious influence.'

'All these years we've lived here,' she said, refusing to rise to the bait. 'And we've never needed chains on the door. Or locks and bolts either. Until now, it seems,' she added pointedly.

'Halcyon times, no doubt,' Adam said silkily, also refusing to be drawn. 'But nothing lasts for ever. Real life has a nasty habit of pushing itself even into idyllic backwaters like this. As you discovered earlier today.'

'I really don't need to be reminded.' She watched him put the last touches to the chain. 'But I suppose you mean to be kind.'

'My intentions are of the purest.' He bent and examined his handiwork. 'As I said, you need a friend.'

'That's very obliging of you,' she said. 'But perhaps I have enough friends already.'

'Then what are you doing here alone?' Adam straightened, his blue eyes fastening intently on her flushed and stormy face.

The words had been quietly, almost gently spoken, but she felt them cut into her like a knife. Was that the kind of pitiable figure she presented? she asked herself. The archetypal spinster and her cat?

She lifted her chin. 'Actually, I made a choice. I wanted to spend some time alone for a change.'

'And then I came along and destroyed the tranquil moment,' Adam suggested drily. 'Is that what you were going to say?'

Tara bit her lip. 'Yes—as it happens. And you still haven't explained what brought you here.'

'Perhaps I too have a secret craving for solitude,' he said. 'Maybe we both drew the short straw this weekend.'

Tara raised her eyebrows. 'A craving for solitude when you're about to be married? The lady has my sympathy.'

'No need.' He shook his head. 'I plan to spend the rest of my life within very positive reach of her.'

'She must be incredibly trusting,' Tara persisted, despising herself. 'Letting you rove round the country like this.'

His blue gaze watched her gravely. 'She has no reason to doubt me. And never will have.'

Her face burned suddenly as she remembered how he had stepped away from her need, her conscious yearning.

She drew a quick breath. 'What a paragon you are.' There was acid in the jeer.

'No,' he said levelly. 'Just an ordinary guy who by some miracle has found the one woman to fulfil his dreams and desires.' He paused. 'Who wouldn't stick like glue in those circumstances?'

Pain twisted inside her. Her voice sounded ragged. 'I—I have no answer to that.'

She turned and went back into the dining room. Adam followed, standing in the doorway.

'Well, you certainly didn't come down to relax,' he commented, brows raised.

'I like to work,' she said shortly.

'Work is fine,' he agreed. 'As long as it doesn't become a barrier.'

'A barrier to what?' Tara dipped her roller into the paint.

'To thinking—feeling—being.'

'Heavens.' Her small laugh was metallic. 'Maybe you should give up being a draughtsman and apply yourself to human psychology instead.'

'Perhaps I will,' he said, unperturbed. 'In the meantime, why don't I get another roller and start on the ceiling?'

Tara paused, startled. 'Thanks for the offer,' she said after a moment. 'But I can manage.'

She'd expected him to argue the point, but instead he simply shrugged, and said, 'Fine. In that case I'll get back to my own painting.'

It was absurd to feel disappointed, but she did.

She saw him presently on the jetty, seated at his easel, with Buster stretched out beside him.

I can't miss him, she thought. He's right in my line of vision.

When it was mid-afternoon, she made tea, and piled a plate with cheese and pickle sandwiches. She loaded a tray and carried it out of the house.

Adam observed her approach with lifted brows. 'What's this?' he asked coolly. 'Has peace suddenly broken out?'

Tara bit her lip. 'I—I realise I wasn't very gracious

about the chain. And it was good of you to take the trouble.'

He eyed her for a moment. 'If you're still worried about where the chain came from, I promise I'll fit another.'

'Thank you.' Tara hesitated. 'I suppose I'm nit-picking, but old Mr Dean was such a private person. He'd have hated a stranger going into his house and borrowing anything, whether he needed it or not.'

'So I gather.' Adam's tone was suddenly remote, and although he was still looking at her Tara had the odd impression that he wasn't seeing her at all.

She moved slightly, restively, and saw his attention click back into the usual faint mockery.

He took one of the sandwiches. 'Well, on your own head be it. You know what they say about stray dogs— feed them and they'll never leave.'

'Buster isn't a stray.' She offered the recumbent hound a crust, which he accepted civilly. 'He obviously has a terrific pedigree.'

Adam said gently, 'And I wasn't talking about Buster.'

There was a silence which she sought, hastily, to fill. 'May I look at your painting?'

'Of course.' He got up, stretching lazily. She saw the ripple of muscle under the faded navy polo shirt and swiftly looked away, turning her attention to the watercolour on the easel.

She knew from the site he'd chosen that he could only be painting Silver Creek House, and as he'd claimed to be a draughtsman she was expecting something stark and representational, drawn with detailed accuracy.

But it wasn't like that at all. The house itself was

little more than an impression, masked behind a soft golden haze, guarded by the tall slender lines of the silver birches.

A dream place, Tara thought wonderingly, like the castle of some sleeping princess, barely glimpsed, but never to be forgotten. And, in a way, the image she carried in her own mind when she was at a distance from it.

'You're disappointed?' He'd noticed her silence.

She mustered a smile. 'On the contrary. Surprised, maybe,' she added.

'You thought I'd be doing it by numbers?' His answering grin was relaxed.

'I'm not that much of a philistine.' She moved away, sinking down on a sun-warmed slab of paving stone to drink her tea. Staring at the pattern on the mug until it blurred, she said, 'What made you choose our house as a subject?' She gestured at the river. 'I mean there's so much gorgeous scenery locally.'

He shrugged. 'Perhaps I wanted a souvenir of this place in particular.' He glanced at the river, to where *Caroline* rode at anchor. 'Something to take with me when I leave.'

Her heart seemed to skip a beat. That sounded as if he were going quite soon. Which was exactly what she wanted, she reminded herself quickly.

She said brightly, 'Are you going to paint Dean's Mooring, too?'

'The other side of the coin?' His voice was suddenly bleak. 'No, I don't think so.'

He drained his mug and replaced it on the tray.

'Thank you for that.' His smile glinted at her. 'You're a mass of surprises.'

And I could say the same for you, she thought. The

mocking charm, the gut-wrenching physical attraction, and the flashes of real kindness he'd shown her were only part of the picture. Occasionally, like a cloud crossing the sun, she caught a glimpse of a darker side to Adam Barnard.

'You're welcome.' She got lightly to her feet. 'I can't wait to see the finished painting,' she added as she picked up the tray.

The smile lingered. 'I'm flattered. I hope you'll like it.'

She could feel his eyes on her as she walked back to the house.

She fed Melusine and then went back to her work, aware that every time she passed the window her gaze was being drawn instinctively to his seated figure.

I'm becoming obsessive, she derided herself crossly, and was even angrier to find herself disappointed when eventually he packed up and returned to *Caroline*.

She had, she realised, been half expecting a knock on the door. A quick check on the progress she was making.

Which made her every kind of fool, because Adam had offered friendship, nothing more, and friends did not spend every moment in each other's pockets.

When she too decided to call it a day, she could feel well pleased with her efforts, she decided, looking round. She cleaned the roller and tray, leaving everything ready for the morning.

Usually she would not have bothered to change, knowing there was no one around to see her, but this evening she found herself upstairs, showering swiftly and discarding her paint-spattered clothes for a pair of cream cotton trousers and a simple tunic top in king-fisher-blue.

Pathetic or what? she disparaged herself as she gave her hair a vigorous brushing.

Downstairs again, she cooked pasta, fried strips of bacon and tomatoes to add to it, then covered the entire dish in grated cheese before popping it under the grill.

She'd made enough for two, she realised wryly, but it seemed that tonight she was going to be the only taker.

While the cheese was melting and browning, Tara poured some Chablis into a glass and wandered outside with it. It was what she did on every fine evening, she reminded herself, a touch defensively, so there was no need to feel self-conscious as she strolled down to the water's edge.

The sun was low in the sky, and there was a faint wind blowing from the water. On board *Caroline* a lamp had been lit in the saloon, and she thought she could see movement.

She could certainly hear something. Music, she thought, played softly enough for her to have to strain her ears to catch the melody. Poignant, and hauntingly romantic, it caught at her memory, taking her back to a concert of English music she'd attended the previous summer.

Delius, she thought, as the main theme swelled to a crescendo. 'A Walk to the Paradise Garden'.

The cool wine was like balm to the burn in her throat as she stood, listening, and watching Adam's boat with an intensity that made her tremble.

The soft chords were like a siren's call, summoning her across the water. Her family's dinghy was tied up a few feet away. It would be the work of minutes to go to him.

He'd offered her friendship, after all, she argued silently. Why shouldn't she take him up on that offer? Share his music. Invite him to share her food again. Even—share her bed...

Her heart seemed to stop for a minute.

Because that isn't enough, she realised rawly, and it never will be. Because I want to share his life—all of him—and he belongs to someone else.

I could probably steal him for a while. Tell him that we're ships passing in the night. That I'll make no demands. There'll be no after-shock to mess up his chosen life.

But if we play the seduction game I could lose out terribly—irretrievably. And the hurt of it might be more than I am able to bear.

After Jack, I swore I'd never be at any man's mercy again. I have to remember that. I can't let myself be tempted by kindness.

The music had changed as she walked back to the house. Now it was the wistful resonance of 'The Banks of Green Willow' that followed her like a long-remembered regret.

And lingered in her head long after she had closed the door and tried to banish it.

The next day would be a totally new start, she promised herself, staring sleeplessly into the darkness that night.

It was sad—it was laughable—it was ludicrous—this hunger for a man she hardly knew. It also had to stop.

And why couldn't any of Becky's suitable and respectable candidates have fired her senses and created the same fever in her blood? she raged inwardly. Oh, God, it was so unfair.

But none of Becky's offerings had ever been lying a stone's throw away from her on a moonlit river, she reminded herself wryly. So near—and yet a world distant. The world to which he would soon be returning.

And she had a life to go back to as well. A loving family. A career that many people would envy. She was young and healthy, and one of these days or years a man would come into her life who was free, and with whom she could build something lasting.

It was an excellent, positive plan—and why it should shriek 'second-best' was something that Tara did not want to contemplate.

At least, not if she was ever to sleep again, she thought, turning over and closing her eyes with determination.

In the morning, the weather had changed. Tara opened her curtains on grey, depressing swathes of mist-drizzle blowing across in front of the window.

A day to stay close to home and not let even the imagination wander, she told herself as she showered and dressed.

Melusine, who loathed wet weather, recoiled in disgust when the back door was opened, and had to be pushed, gently but firmly, outside. She reappeared almost immediately, sitting on the kitchen window-sill, pulling furious faces as Tara boiled an egg and made toast and coffee. Re-admitted, she ignored the placatory saucer of milk Tara had put down for her, and retired to the dresser to sulk.

'Please yourself entirely,' Tara told her, and went on with her own breakfast.

However drab the weather outside, indoors the dining room, at least, gave an illusion of sunshine, she decided with a stirring of pleasure as she inspected yesterday's handiwork with a critical eye.

She was just about to climb her stepladder and start again when there was a knock at the front door.

For a second she was tempted not to answer, but reason told her it was better to behave normally.

She had fastened the chain the night before, so she opened the door to its restricted limit and peeped round it.

Buster was sitting there, looking glum, a piece of paper attached to his collar. When he saw Tara, he allowed his tail one ingratiating thump.

'What on earth...?' Tara detached the chain and opened the door fully. As she bent to retrieve the paper Buster licked her hand and looked soulful.

It was only a brief message. 'I can't do my kind of painting, so please may we both help with yours?'

Oh *hell*, thought Tara. Now what do I do?

She looked at Buster. 'And I suppose you're waiting for a reply?'

'I think that might be pushing it.' Adam appeared apparently from nowhere, a waterproof slung across his shoulders. 'So you'd better tell me instead.

'If it's no, we can take it,' he added. 'But maybe I should mention that a boat, however comfortable, shrinks to the size of a shoebox in this weather. And Buster is claustrophobic.'

Tara sighed. 'Then you'd better come in. For Buster's sake.' She paused. 'Did you teach him that pleading look?'

He grinned at her. 'I knew that would soften your heart. With a little more practice he'll be irresistible.'

He was not, she thought, the only one.

The rain had darkened Adam's hair, and there were drops of water on his face and clinging to his lashes.

She found herself thinking how cool his skin would feel if she touched it with her lips.

He took off the waterproof and hung it up. Under it he was wearing jeans, and a faded sweatshirt that emphasised the spread of his shoulders.

He turned, his brows lifted in query as he met her gaze. 'Shall we make a start?'

'Yes—of course.' Flustered, Tara led the way into the dining room.

'It looks good.' Adam gazed around him, nodding with appreciation. 'My offer to paint the ceiling still stands—unless there's something else you'd prefer me to do?'

'No—oh, no. The ceiling would be fine.' She paused. 'Would you like coffee before you start?'

'I have this Puritan ethic,' he said. 'I believe in working before I get a reward.'

Tara forced a smile. 'Some reward—a cup of coffee.'

'Ah,' he said, softly. 'But if I work really hard, maybe the offer will improve.'

Tara said, 'I'll get the ceiling emulsion,' and fled.

In spite of her misgivings, the morning passed without a hitch, Adam proving adept with a paint roller. And at lunchtime he proved equally skilful in the kitchen, producing a deliciously filling Spanish omelette for them both.

'I'm overcome with admiration,' Tara said as she finished the last scrap. 'You must do a lot of cooking.'

He grimaced. 'I rarely get the opportunity.'

Presumably because his fiancée considered that her own prerogative, Tara told herself without pleasure. She decided to switch to a safer topic.

'I think the rain is stopping,' she remarked, directing her gaze away from him to the window.

'Whether it is or not, I'll have to take Buster for a run.' Adam bent to fondle the dog's ears. 'Won't I, old boy?'

'He's been so good. He must be really bored, shut up here while we paint.'

'He's fine, as long as he's with people he likes.' Adam smiled at her. 'He got pretty excited last evening when he saw you on the riverbank. He thought you were coming to pay us a visit. I thought maybe you were there to complain about the music. I hope it didn't disturb you.'

Not in the way you'd suppose, Tara thought.

Aloud, she said, 'No—I enjoyed what I could hear of it. Especially the Delius. It took me back to a concert I went to last summer.'

'At the Festival Hall?' Adam's brows lifted. 'I was there too.' His smile widened, teasing her. 'You see—we're not really new friends at all. We've been involved for a year already.'

'Not,' she said, 'an argument that would stand close examination.' She pushed back her chair and rose. 'I'll wash up, and then get on with painting the woodwork. Thanks for all your help. I'll be finished in half the time now.'

Adam got to his feet too. 'Do I take it you're dispensing with my services?' He was still smiling, but his eyes were grave.

Tara shrugged, trying for nonchalance. 'Well, you must have plenty of other things to do. You're on holiday, after all.'

'So I am,' he said. 'A working holiday, like yours.' He walked unhurriedly round the table and stood in front of her.

Too close, she thought, for comfort.

He said, 'Tara, why do you want to push me away all the time?'

'It's not that—really.' Her protest sounded small and rather breathless. 'I don't want to be a nuisance—making calls on your time.'

'You're not.' He reached out and brushed a strand of hair gently back from her forehead.

The kind of casual caress, she thought raggedly, that he'd have bestowed on either of the animals, and felt her body arch and stir with the same feral pleasure.

'So am I allowed to claim my reward?' The blue eyes held hers, watchful, even faintly amused, as if he'd sensed her instinctive reaction.

Her throat seemed to close up. 'That would rather depend—on what you want.'

'Nothing too drastic.' Quite slowly and deliberately, he clasped his hands behind his back.

As if, she thought, staring fixedly at a spot of paint on his sweatshirt, he was keeping them out of possible mischief. But if that was meant to be a gesture of reassurance then it had misfired badly. And had come far too late.

Despite the layers of clothing that divided them, she could feel the warmth of his body reaching her. Absorb the clean, male scent of him through every pore. Common sense suggested she should step backwards—remove herself from the danger zone. But for the life of her she could not summon the will to move.

'I'd simply like you to go out for a drink with me tonight.' His voice seemed to reach her from a vast distance. 'There's a folk band playing at the Black Horse in the village. I thought we could go there.'

She tried to think of an excuse, but nothing remotely convincing came to mind, and nothing less than total conviction would do. She knew that. Because it was important not to let him guess just how shaken she was by his proximity.

Being alone with him was not an option she should pursue, but, on the other hand, a pub in the village was probably just about as public—and as safe—as it could get.

She didn't put her own hands behind her back. That, she thought, would have been too obvious.

Instead, she picked up her used plate and cutlery from the table and carried them over to the sink. Out of harm's way.

Over her shoulder, she gave Adam a brief, non-committal smile.

'Thank you,' she said. 'I'd like that.'

'Then I'll pick you up about eight.' His voice sounded quiet, almost formal.

She heard him cross the room, the dog padding beside him, and go down the passage. Then the closing of the front door.

She leaned against the sink and bowed her head.

She thought, What have I done? And, dear God, what am I doing?

But there was no answer in the enfolding silence. No sound at all, except the frantic drumming of her own heart.

CHAPTER SIX

'IT ISN'T,' Tara said, 'as if it was a real date. So it really doesn't matter what I wear. Does it?'

Melusine, lying on the bed, her paws neatly disposed under her, opened her eyes and squinted with the weary scorn of one who'd heard it all before. As indeed she had. Several times.

'And you're no help,' Tara added, holding yet another pair of jeans and top in front of her and glaring at her reflection.

She didn't wish to appear as if she'd dressed up for the occasion, treating it as some kind of special thing.

On the other hand she didn't want to look as if she'd been dragged through a hedge backwards either.

And she'd brought no going-out clothes with her for the very good reason she'd planned on spending her evenings at home.

So much for planning, she thought, with a sigh. Of course she could always make an excuse—invent a headache when Adam called for her. And she could also visualise the cynical disbelief that would twist his mouth if she did any such thing.

She sighed again, and tossed the clothes she was holding on to the bed, just missing Melusine, who gave her an affronted stare.

'You don't walk in my shoes, so don't judge me,' Tara told her, running a distracted hand through her hair.

Of course there were always the things that she'd left

in her old room, she realised, frowning. They weren't new by any means, just oddments that had accumulated over the years, but there might be something that deserved another outing.

A swift rummage through the wardrobe produced a button-through denim skirt, flaring to mid-calf, and a blue and white striped shirt.

At least tonight she would look more like a woman and less like a painter and decorator. Though maybe overalls and a blow torch might be safer gear, she acknowledged, her lips twisting.

In her mother's room, she found a dark blue knitted jacket and a pair of plain navy pumps.

When she was dressed, and her newly washed hair had been dried to curve smoothly and silkily round her face, she could even be moderately pleased with the overall effect. She applied a dusting of colour to her eyelids and cheekbones, and painted her mouth a soft rose.

She was just descending the stairs when she heard Adam's knock, and drew a deep, steadying breath before she opened the door.

His brows lifted when he saw her, and he whistled softly and appreciatively. 'You look terrific.'

'You're not so bad yourself,' she returned, keeping her tone light. Because actually he was breathtaking, in beautifully cut dark trousers, topped by a black sweater, and a jacket in a fine black and white tweed that looked expensive and Italian.

She felt hunger twist inside her, a cold, desolate thing that could never be satisfied.

He was looking down at her feet. 'Are you going to be able to walk to the village in those shoes?'

'I'm not even going to try. We'll go in my car.' She

met his gaze with something of a challenge. She'd decided while she was dressing that being at the controls of a vehicle seemed a safer bet than a long walk home in the moonlight.

'In other words you plan to keep a cool head this evening.' He sounded amused, but not put out.

'I usually do.' She noticed he hadn't tried to talk her out of it. She also noticed Buster sitting in the doorway. 'Is he coming with us?'

'No, I thought I'd leave him here, if that's all right with you.'

'You'd better ask Melusine,' she retorted.

'Oh, I think the truce is holding.' He pointed Buster in the direction of the kitchen, and the dog trotted off obediently. 'Have you locked the back door?'

Tara tutted. 'How did silly little me manage till you came along?' she sighed. 'Yes, it's locked, and bolted too. And I've checked the windows.'

'Leaving me to check my words for any hint of male chauvinism,' he said drily. 'Shall we go?'

'We'd better. The pub gets very busy at holiday times.'

But when they got there she found he'd booked a table.

'How did you manage this?' Tara slid into her seat, noting that the bar was already filling up.

'I found a phone box when I was out with Buster. I hope you haven't eaten already.'

'No, I haven't, and I'm starving.' Tara took the menu he was handing her with a thankful heart.

Adam's lips twitched. 'You're amazing. You look as if a breath of wind could blow you away, yet you really enjoy your food.'

She laughed back at him. 'That's—' Then stopped

dead, as she realised what she'd been about to say. *That's what Jack used to say.*

Only, 'You eat like a horse and never put on a pound,' had been his actual, faintly carping comment.

'That's what?' Adam prompted.

'That's—not a very fashionable way to be,' Tara said swiftly. 'Everyone seems to be on some kind of diet these days.'

'That's true,' he said. 'But not what you really started out to say. Is it?'

She buried her nose in the menu, hoping her faint flush wouldn't be noticed. 'I don't know what you're talking about. And I'd like the spiced chicken, with sauté potatoes and a green salad, please.'

'I'll have the beef and Guinness casserole,' Adam decided. He looked at her. 'Are you going to permit yourself one unit of alcohol, or are you scared it might make your tongue run away with you?' he added silkily.

'Not at all.' She handed her menu back. 'A dry white wine spritzer, please.'

His absence at the bar gave her a chance to recover her composure. Keep the conversation general, she adjured herself silently. Don't let this man under your guard, or he could be there, in your heart, for the rest of your life.

Perhaps she was one of those women always doomed to choose men with whom there was no future, she thought bleakly.

The folk band arrived at this juncture, and began to set up, so when Adam returned to their table it was easy to dive into a discussion about musical preferences—on which they seemed far too closely attuned for comfort, Tara decided uneasily.

The Black Horse was known for the quality of its cooking, so the food, when it came, provided another safe topic.

Her confused emotional state notwithstanding, Tara ate every scrap, including the excellent pear tart that both she and Adam chose for dessert.

And once the music started it wasn't possible to talk much at all. The lead singers, a girl in a broad-brimmed black hat and a tall man with a ponytail and a crimson brocade waistcoat, had good voices, and excellent backing from traditional Irish instruments. They also had a beguiling way at the microphone, so that Tara found, almost in spite of herself, she was joining in the communal efforts with everyone else, conscious of Adam's pleasant baritone beside her.

And when the girl sang, unaccompanied, 'The Londonderry Air', dedicating it to the cause of peace in Northern Ireland, a pin could have been heard to drop.

The time seemed to fly past.

'It's over too soon,' Tara sighed, as the band, vociferously applauded, sang their last encore.

'It doesn't have to be,' Adam said. 'May I offer you a nightcap on *Caroline*?'

She could hardly plead tiredness after her previous remark, she realised vexedly. Besides, she had to admit to a certain curiosity. No doubt there would be pictures of his fiancée and other clues to his life she could pick up, so that when he went, he wouldn't linger in her mind like an enigma.

Once I've solved his mystery, she thought, I can be at peace again.

It was a quiet drive back to Silver Creek. Adam seemed lost in thought, and she was reluctant to disturb his reverie. In any case, she had plenty to think about herself.

As she drew up she could hear Buster barking, a lonely, almost frantic sound which made the hairs on the back of her neck prickle.

As she unlocked the front door a terrified Melusine appeared from the darkness like a bullet from a gun, leaping on to Tara's shoulder and wrapping herself round her neck like a trembling scarf.

'Sweetheart, what is it?' Tara tried to detach her pet's claws from her jacket, but Melusine clung like a burr. 'Buster must have frightened her.' She turned angrily on Adam. 'I knew we shouldn't have left them together.'

'Then why isn't he chasing her now?' Adam went past her and into the kitchen. Buster, still barking, was lying with his muzzle pressed against the back door.

'Something's upset them both,' Adam said, frowning. 'Have you got a flashlight?'

'It's on a hook inside the pantry door.'

He found it, and, coaxing Buster away from his vigil, unfastened the back door and let himself out.

'Dogs and cats simply don't get on,' she insisted stubbornly, shivering in the sudden draught of cool night air. 'And that's all there is to it.'

'Is it?' His voice came to her grimly out of the darkness. 'Come and have a look at this.'

Still wearing Melusine, she joined him, Buster leaping excitedly beside her until Adam quietened him with a word.

'What am I supposed to be seeing?' she began, then gasped as she saw the deep gouges in the stout old wooden frame, and in the edge of the door itself. 'What's that?'

'I'd say someone had been trying to jemmy it open.' Adam's voice was harsh. 'Fortunately it's a good, strong door, and there was the added disincentive of a dog in the house.'

Tara's heart seemed to stop. She put out a hand, touching the splintered wood, then recoiled.

'God,' she said huskily. 'I feel sick.'

His arm was round her like an iron bar. 'Breathe deeply,' he ordered. 'Nothing happened. Everything's fine.'

The breath was rasping in her chest. She turned, beating at him with clenched fists. 'What are you talking about? Someone tried to break in. That's nothing?'

'It could have been much worse,' he said curtly.

'That's easy for you to say.' She dragged herself free and confronted him, her breasts rising and falling stormily. 'It's not your place that's been under attack. Although you have a pretty casual attitude to other people's property anyway. You seem prepared to stroll in and help yourself to anything that suits you.'

He was very still. 'Are you still wound up about that bloody door chain?'

'I think I've a right to be.' Her voice rose. 'Just look at the facts. You arrive from nowhere—take over a private mooring—behave as if you own the place—inveigle yourself into my house—and within a matter of days someone tries to break in.'

'After I've cleared the way by taking you out for the evening, of course.' His tone was icy with contempt. 'You forgot to mention that bit.'

'I haven't forgotten a bloody thing, believe me,' she said thickly.

There was a silence, then he sighed. 'Tara—you're upset, and you have every reason to be so, but you're not thinking rationally. If I was setting you up, why would I leave Buster on guard?'

'A smokescreen,' she flared back at him defiantly.

'Oh, for God's sake,' he said wearily. 'That's crazy, and you know it.'

'I don't know anything,' she said, her voice shaking. 'And especially I don't know anything about you, Adam—who you are—where you come from.' She took a breath. 'All I do know is you're here—and everything's different suddenly—and I don't want it to be,' she added on a little wail. 'I want you away from here. Away from me.'

'Then I'll try not to distress you any more than necessary.' His voice was terse. 'Are you going to tell the police?'

'Tomorrow—perhaps—I don't know.' Her hands twisted together. 'After all, nothing really did happen.'

He nodded. 'Will you be all right? If it's any comfort, I doubt if your unwanted visitor will come back.'

'I'll be fine.' She detached Melusine from her shoulder, holding the cat in front of her like a shield.

'Then I'll go.' He paused. 'I'll talk to you tomorrow, Tara. It will all seem better in daylight, I promise.'

'No,' she said. 'I don't think it will change a thing.' She held out a hand. 'May I have my flashlight, please?'

He surrendered it without a word and she stepped backwards into the kitchen, leaving him alone in the darkness. She heard Buster's puzzled whimper as she pushed the door shut with her foot.

She put Melusine down while she relocked the door and manoeuvred the heavy bolts into place. Not easy when her hands—her whole body—were trembling so much.

This house had always been her sanctuary—her place of safety. Now, suddenly, all security seemed to have flown, and there was danger instead. Not least the danger posed by the man whom she knew, with total certainty, was still standing silently outside.

Because although she might have been able to exclude him physically from the house, it would not be so easy to banish him from her heart and mind. As long as night followed day he would be there in her consciousness, irrevocably and for ever.

Yet how could she trust him when instinct told her she was only seeing half the man?

She sank down on the rocking chair, lifting Melusine on to her lap.

'Oh, baby,' she whispered, burying her face in the silky fur. 'What am I going to do?'

In spite of her rejection of him, she half expected to find Adam on the doorstep next morning. He would not, she thought, take his dismissal easily.

But there was no sign of him. In fact, *Caroline* looked deserted in the morning sunshine.

Breakfast finished, she drove to the village and reported the attempted break-in. The police were kind, but made it clear there was little they could do, as it was unlikely the would-be burglar would have left fingerprints or other clues. They were rather more interested when she mentioned the visit from the supposed antiques dealer, but overall she was made to feel she'd had a lucky escape and should count her blessings.

One pertinent point she'd failed to mention, of course, as she realised on her way home, was Adam's presence.

A night's rest and reflection had convinced her that

he'd had nothing to do with the break-in and her accusations had been prompted by shock. But all the unanswered questions still remained.

The previous evening he'd been a relaxed and amusing companion, attentive to her enjoyment but without fuss. She'd felt warmed to her soul. Happier than she'd been since...

Her mind closed off. Perhaps the would-be burglar had done her a favour, she thought. Because if she'd gone for that nightcap on *Caroline* heaven knew what might have happened. But it could have been something to regret as long as she lived.

And I already have enough regrets, she told herself bleakly.

There was no easel on the jetty when she got back. No music floating across the water, or wistful dog with a message tucked into his collar either.

She supposed she ought to finish painting the dining room, but the plan held little appeal.

It was a Bank Holiday, after all, so why shouldn't she take some time off along with the rest of the nation? Enjoy the fine weather and her unexpected privacy all at the same time?

She'd come across one of her old bikinis while she'd been rooting through her wardrobe the night before.

She changed, looking with disfavour at the pallor of her skin, and slid her feet into faded espadrilles. Then she collected a lounger from the shed at the rear and took it to a sheltered spot at the side of the house furthest from Dean's Mooring.

Luxury, she told herself as she stretched out, relishing the sun's warmth. This is definitely my best idea of the day.

But somehow she couldn't settle. The book she'd

chosen—a much-hyped bestseller—failed to engage her attention, and there seemed nothing on the radio worth listening to either. The trouble was she was constantly on the alert, she realised unhappily. Waiting—listening for Adam's return.

Eventually she said, 'Oh, this is ridiculous,' and stood up, reaching for the filmy white shirt she wore as a cover-up and looking speculatively across at *Caroline*.

Of course, Adam could be right there on board, maybe sleeping off a post-tiff hangover.

I'm flattering myself, she thought. Why should he get blasted because he and I have a row?

Nevertheless, she owed him some kind of an apology for last night, and she knew it. And it was quite easy. All she had to do was go on board and say, Hi, is it too late for that nightcap? Or one of a dozen or so other little speeches which explained that the attempted break-in had sent her head temporarily into orbit and her tongue had gone with it. Or something.

She would also mention that she was going home the following day and had come to say goodbye. Because that, she had come to see, was the only sane and sensible course of action.

She walked down the jetty and paused, cupping her hands to her mouth.

'Hi, there, on *Caroline*. Permission to come aboard?'

But there was no answer. Not even a welcoming bark from Buster.

She moved closer, called again, but her words fell into the silence.

It wasn't a conscious decision, but somehow she was on *Caroline*'s deck and opening the door which led to the companionway. She descended, and stood looking around her. Compared to poor little *Naiad* this was a floating palace. There were two cabins, both for double occupation, a beautifully fitted galley, and a saloon panelled in some pale wood.

It was such a waste for this lovely boat to be moored here. She could imagine sailing downstream to the estuary, and out into the open sea. Could hear the splash of real waves against the bow and breathe the clean, salt-laden wind.

She could imagine cooking meals in the galley and taking her turn in the wheelhouse. At night, dropping anchor in some sheltered bay and sleeping in the wide, comfortable bunk in the main cabin, with Adam's arms around her.

Dream on, she thought, biting her lip. That was someone else's perquisite.

She trailed back to the saloon. There was cushioned seating round the bulkheads, as well as a couple of easy chairs, a chart locker and a large fold-down table, currently covered in big sheets of paper.

More sketches, she realised. Adam might have been wasting his sailing opportunities, but certainly not his time.

She wandered over and had a look. Not Silver Creek House this time, she saw, but a very different subject. A row of terraced cottages, almost like a mews development, with window boxes, gables, and neatly parked cars.

Tara wrinkled her nose. It was impeccably, even brilliantly drawn, but it didn't have a fraction of the flair and imagination of his watercolour. Yet at the same time it seemed oddly familiar.

She looked at the next sheet. An alternative view of the same thing—a side elevation, she supposed. And,

on a third sheet, no sketches at all, but a detailed plan
drawn to scale. Not simply one row of houses, but
three, built round an open square to the rear. And in
one corner of the paper, plainly printed, the legend
'Dean's Mooring Development'.

Tara stared at it until the letters began to blur and
dance. She was gripping the edge of the table so tightly
that her knuckles had turned white.

He'd called himself a draughtsman, she thought
dazedly. But that wasn't the half of it. Adam Barnard
was an architect, and one who'd come to Silver Creek
for a very definite purpose.

She dropped the plan back on the table as if it was
contaminated.

If he bought Dean's Mooring and converted it into
holiday cottages then Silver Creek would be ruined. Its
whole character and ambience would change disas-
trously. There'd be constant traffic noise, she thought,
staring with loathing at the parked cars on the first
drawing. Not to mention more and more boats on the
river. Landing facilities would have to be improved,
and the access road widened.

And, quite apart from losing its peace and privacy,
her parents' house would nosedive in value. Although
that, she knew, wouldn't matter to them as much as the
loss of their seclusion.

It would be the end of an era, she thought numbly.

There was a portfolio under the table. Maybe there
were more drawings in there. More clues to exactly
what he was planning—and how far those plans were
advanced.

She knelt, pulling at the strings with clumsy fingers.
But there were no plans, simply watercolours. Local

scenes and, on top, the most recent. His painting of
Silver Creek House.

Tara took it out and looked at it. How could he paint
the fragile beauty of its environment with such sensi-
tivity when he was planning to destroy it? she wondered, her throat tightening painfully.

But perhaps that was why he'd wanted it, as a souvenir, she thought—then paused, staring down at it, her
eyes widening. Because this was not the painting she'd
seen at the quay, she realised in shocked disbelief. It
had been changed...

The house was still shrouded in golden light, but at
an upstairs window the veil had parted to reveal the
naked figure of a girl—slender and pagan, her face
lifted to the sun and her hands cupping her breasts. A
study in warm, uninhibited sexuality. *Her* study.

My God, she thought. He saw me that morning. He
actually saw me.

A few minutes ago, poring over the plans, she'd been
ice-cold, but now she burned.

Somewhere—in some far distant level of consciousness—she heard thudding noises, then furious barking
from Buster as he hurled himself down the companionway and into the saloon, with Adam one step behind
him. Tara got slowly to her feet to face them, the painting in her hand.

Buster skidded to a halt beside her, eyes liquid with
pleased recognition, waiting for her acknowledgement,
for the caressing hand.

But Tara could not move. She could only look across
the saloon at Adam, her eyes blazing in her white face,
watching the amused appreciation in his smile as he
assimilated what she was wearing freeze and die on
his lips.

There was a short but telling silence, then he said quietly, 'Welcome to *Caroline*. I'm glad you've made yourself at home.'

She said thickly, 'Are you indeed? Are you quite sure of that?'

She turned back to the table, sweeping the plans and drawings to the floor with one quick, angry gesture.

She said, 'You know I won't let you do this.'

'How do you propose to stop me?' The man who'd turned her blood to fire had vanished, leaving a remote stranger in his place.

Tara lifted her chin. 'We're going to buy Dean's Mooring,' she said.

'Indeed,' he said gravely. 'Is that the royal ''we''?'

'My family,' she said. 'And myself.'

'You're sure it's for sale?'

'Of course. I'm going to speak to the solicitor handling old Mr Dean's estate after the weekend.'

'I'll save you the trouble. Dean's Mooring is owned by the old man's grandson, and he isn't selling.'

Tara stared at him. 'Mr Dean had no family.'

'Wrong,' Adam said harshly. 'He had a daughter, but they quarrelled and he never spoke to her again. When she wrote and told him she had a son, he made a will leaving everything to the boy he would never meet.'

Her mouth was suddenly dry. 'How do you know so much about it?'

His smile was just a grim twist of the lips. 'How do you think?' He paused. 'While you were going through my papers just now, you might have noticed my initials on the plans—ADB. Standing for Adam Dean Barnard.'

He heard her shocked gasp and nodded coldly. 'Precisely, Miss Lyndon. I'm Ambrose Dean's grandson. Dean's Mooring belongs to me. And, as you can see, I have my own ideas about its future.'

CHAPTER SEVEN

'YOU look surprised.' Adam's mocking voice seemed to reach Tara from a far distance. 'You much preferred to write me off as an intruder and a thief, didn't you, sweetheart?'

'And instead it's just plain "liar",' she said. And Peeping Tom, she thought, her throat contracting.

'I never lied to you, Tara.'

'You let me think...'

He lifted a hand. 'That's not the same thing at all. I gave you endless hints, but you never picked up on any of them.'

'You pretended you'd come here for peace and quiet,' she said bitterly. 'And all the time you were planning to wreck Silver Creek. Destroy it.'

'There's a demand for riverside development.' Adam shrugged, his face hard. 'Why shouldn't I supply it?'

'Because Dean's Mooring was your grandfather's home—part of your heritage.'

'Now there's an emotive word,' he said softly. 'A cruel, selfish old man shuts himself off from the world, and I'm supposed to turn his refuge into some kind of shrine?' He shook his head. 'I don't think so.'

He paused. 'Or are you really more worried about your own family monument over there, and the effect development might have on its value?'

'My parents will be concerned, naturally.' Tara spoke with dignity.

'Then maybe instead of buying they might consider

selling,' he drawled. 'The whole river frontage would be an even better proposition.'

Tara gasped. 'They'd see you in hell first.' She brushed past him, making for the companionway and the deck beyond.

'Wait,' he said. 'I think you have something of mine.'

She realised she was still holding the watercolour. She flourished it at him contemptuously. 'What—this little piece of second-rate pornography?'

She saw his mouth tighten—a muscle flicker in his tanned cheek.

'You're quite a multi-talented man, Mr Barnard,' she said. 'But you don't belong here. And nor do your tacky little tourist boxes. So why don't you just clear out—and find somewhere else to pollute!'

She spun round, and went up the companionway fast. Buster gave a joyous bark and bounded after her, impeding Adam, who stumbled and swore.

By the time he gained the deck, she was at the rail.

Adam paused, chest heaving, watching her with wary, narrowed eyes.

He said, 'I'd like my painting back.'

'And I'd like you to leave my parents' house alone— and stop foisting your sick ideas of art on to it,' Tara said, and tore the watercolour across with one scornful gesture.

Adam groaned, and started forward, but she ripped the painting again, and tossed the fragments over the side into the river.

He swore again, eyes closed and head flung back, but this time it sounded like some agonised prayer. He stood for a moment, hands clenched, clearly fighting for control. Then he came towards her.

'Tara—listen to me...' He sounded shaken.

'You haven't a thing to say that I want to hear.' The words were being forged out of the nameless, boundless pain which was consuming her. Out of the shame of knowing that he'd seen her naked at her window—wanting him—offering herself. 'Get out of here. Go back where you came from.'

She drew a swift, harsh breath. 'Oh, God, I should have turned you away that first night—you—you bastard.'

She lifted her hand and hit him across the face, watching with a kind of horror as the marks of her fingers spread across his cheek like a brand. She heard Buster growl softly.

For a long moment she stood motionless, then she took a step backwards, then another, until she was trapped against the rail with no retreat left.

And Adam followed, as she had known he would.

His voice was low, and jagged with ice. 'You've a hot temper there, lady. You need to cool it.'

He swooped, swinging her off her feet and up into his arms. Startled, Tara struggled, but she was no match for his strength.

'Let go of me, damn you. Put me down.' Her eyes dilated as she stared up at him, meeting the sudden predatory glitter in the blue eyes.

'Presently,' he said softly, and his hands slid under the loose shirt, discovering the satin of her half-naked body. She heard his sudden intake of breath, then he bent towards her, his head blotting out the sun.

As his mouth touched hers, her whole body responded sharply, almost convulsively. Her lips parted in acceptance and welcome, and warm liquid heat ran through her like quicksilver.

Her reason might reject him, she realised in some dazed, reeling corner of her mind, but her body was totally enslaved.

The slow, exploratory brush of his fingers against her warm skin was not enough. Her breasts were swelling against the cups of her bikini top, desperate for the caress of his hands or his tongue over her engorged, heated nipples.

She seemed to be flying, she thought deliriously. Soaring. And, she suddenly realised with a choking squeal of alarm, falling too.

She hit the water ungracefully, arms and legs flailing as she was gulped down into the shock of its chill depths. She surfaced again in seconds, coughing, spluttering, and gasping for breath.

She shook the water out of her eyes, peering up at the boat, trying to locate him, because if he was standing there laughing at her she wouldn't rest until he was dead at her feet.

But Adam was nowhere to be seen. Nor was there a friendly boathook in sight, or any helping hand to assist her back on board. She'd been simply left to flounder.

She swam in a wide half-circle away from *Caroline* and the landing stage, making her way to a spot downstream which her family had always used to bathe from. The bank shelved gently into the water, and she waded out through the reeds, the shirt plastered against her body and drops from her drenched hair running down her face, dripping from the end of her nose.

There was water in her ears too, she discovered vengefully, shaking her head to clear the buzzing. But it only got louder.

Tara swung round in time to see *Caroline* moving

away from her erstwhile mooring and out into midstream.

He must have cast off while I was in the water, she thought. I told him to go—and he's going. Just as suddenly as that.

Arms wrapped round her shivering body, she watched *Caroline* round the bend and disappear from view. She wanted to scream childishly, Goodbye and good riddance, but the words wouldn't come.

The only sound that rose in her throat was a sob. And there were tears mingling with the droplets of river water on her face.

She'd imagined he would return that evening, and vengefully rehearsed what she would say. How she would behave. But when night came the mooring was still unoccupied.

In fact, three days went slowly past with no sign of him. And a visit to Hanman and Brough simply confirmed everything he'd told her. Dean's Mooring, she was told kindly but firmly, was not for sale. And an application for planning permission would be made. So that, she realised, was that.

She tried to blot the whole thing out of her mind with work—scrubbing paintwork and floors, cleaning windows, turning out cupboards and laundering curtains and bedding—thus ensuring that when she finally dropped into bed at night she slept like a log. But she couldn't control her dreams. Couldn't block Adam from coming to her each night, or escape the illusion of his hands and mouth caressing her body—his voice whispering words she would never hear except in dreams.

And she woke each morning to the bitter knowledge that she'd been crying.

When she couldn't think of another single job to do in the house she went out in *Naiad*, and spent what she intended to be a day of total relaxation exploring the river, using the engine instead of sail, and revisiting old haunts.

This could be the last time, she realised drearily. She didn't know how her parents would react to Adam's development plans, but they might well decide to cut their losses and sell up while they could. She already knew they were planning to travel more, so perhaps Silver Creek would become just a memory for them all.

She even called in at the marina, but found she was scanning the cluster of boats for the sleek lines of *Caroline*. Having a drink at the bar, greeting people she knew and exchanging news, all the time she was looking past them, searching the laughing, talking groups for one tall figure.

This, she told herself grimly, cannot go on. I won't let it.

Holidays don't suit me, she thought as she sailed slowly back to Silver Creek. Not even working ones. I need to put all this behind me and get back to the real world. Return to work and start dealing with problems I have an outside chance of solving.

Because what has really happened here? I met a man—I was attracted—he was involved elsewhere. A story as old as time, and as predictable.

And he wasn't some mysterious stranger washed up by destiny either. He was here for sound commercial reasons, according to his own reckoning. Anything else was in my imagination.

So, I should call it a day and go back to London.

In any case the weather was changing, she thought, viewing the clouds building up in the west. By the time she rowed herself ashore, the rain was already falling.

'I'll get the show on the road,' she told Melusine. 'While you go outside and behave like a lady.'

Melusine had to be shooed out, and would no doubt spend the minimum time attending to her needs, Tara decided as she flew upstairs and threw her clothes into her travel bag.

The cleaning materials she packed into their box, and she was just emptying the fridge when she realised that nearly half an hour had gone by with no aggrieved mewing for readmittance.

She's probably sulking under the car, Tara thought, grimacing at the rain falling steadily past the kitchen window. She picked up a bag of left-over groceries, and headed for the back door.

'Mel,' she called. 'Don't give me a hard time now...'

And stopped, aware that something was terribly wrong.

It's the car, she thought. It looks—odd—as if it's suddenly started to sink into the ground...

She stared at it, unable for a moment to believe what she was seeing. Then she put the bag down and walked slowly forward, trembling.

Knowing with terrifying certainty that she wouldn't be going back to London, or anywhere else. Not today.

Because someone had slashed all four tyres on her car. Destroyed them beyond repair.

She wrapped her arms round her body, hugging herself fiercely, trying to control the immediate feeling of panic.

First the attempted break-in—and now this. What was happening to her?

Because this was no mindless act by some passing vandal. No one ever came here by chance, she told herself, nausea, scalding and bitter, rising in her throat. No, this had to be deliberate—and deeply vindictive. And done by someone who knew she was here alone.

But not completely alone, she thought, suddenly frantic. There was Melusine—who was missing—nowhere to be seen.

She looked round frantically, calling her name, hearing her voice crack.

The river, she thought, starting to run, an image in her mind of a small struggling figure in the water...

The distant sound of breaking glass stopped her in her tracks.

That came from Dean's Mooring, she thought blankly. Vandals after all, and doing as much damage as possible.

Well, not if I know it.

Recklessly, she took off towards the other house. The front door was standing ajar, and Tara kicked it wide open.

'I know you're in there,' she shouted into the shadowy interior. 'And the police are on their way.'

'Fascinating,' came a familiar drawl. 'What are you planning to accuse me of this time?'

And Adam appeared in the hall, accompanied by Melusine, who was weaving herself rapturously around his legs.

'You?' Tara croaked the word.

'Unfortunately, yes.' He stood, hands on hips, the blue eyes challenging. 'Whom were you expecting?'

'I—I didn't know what to think. I heard glass...'

He nodded expressionlessly. 'I tried to open the kitchen window and the whole thing fell out instead.'

'But where's *Caroline*?'

'The real one or the boat?' He let her digest that for a moment, then added, 'Whatever, they're both elsewhere. This time I used my car.'

'Aren't you the lucky one?' Tara said, between her teeth. 'As I'm sure you know, I can't use mine.'

'You're being too modest,' Adam returned silkily. 'You're not that bad a driver.'

She said unevenly, 'That, damn you, is not what I mean.'

'I'm sorry,' he said. 'I'm not acquainted with the code you're using today.'

'All right.' Chin lifted, she confronted him, her face cold with contempt. 'Someone's slashed the tyres on my car—all of them. I didn't do it, so that rather puts you in the frame—as the only other person around.'

He bent and retrieved Melusine, hoisting her to his shoulder, where she draped herself bonelessly, with an expression of such idiotic bliss that Tara longed to strangle her.

As he straightened, he was frowning. 'When did this happen?'

'Oh, for God's sake—what kind of game are you playing?'

'I could ask you the same,' he came back at her harshly. 'Why in hell should I do such a crazy thing?'

'You threw me in the river,' she defended.

'You asked for it.'

'I could have drowned!'

He laughed. 'Not you, darling. You walk on water.' He paused. 'When did you last see your car intact?'

'Last night, I suppose. I haven't used it today. I—I went out on the river after breakfast. I was planning to leave this evening. Go back to London.'

'I saw your boat had gone,' he said thoughtfully. 'I got here about two hours ago. But I didn't notice anyone hanging around.'

'Why,' she said, 'does that not surprise me?'

Adam looked at her coldly. 'Get one thing straight,' he said. 'I did not damage your bloody car in any way. God forbid I should detain you here any longer than strictly necessary,' he added, with a bite. 'However, I'm prepared to have a look at it—see if any of the tyres can be saved.'

'They can't.'

'And if not,' he continued, as if she hadn't spoken, 'I'll ring the police and the garage for you.'

'Don't tell me,' she said. 'This time you've brought your mobile phone.'

'If you'd prefer to walk to the nearest call box,' he said pleasantly, 'be my guest.'

She bit her lip. 'No—I mean, I'd be—grateful.'

'Can I have that in writing?' He unwound the purring Melusine and handed her back. 'Here,' he said curtly. 'I don't want to be charged with alienation of affections as well.' And he strode off.

Tara stared after him. Only a few days ago he'd held her, touched her with the hands of a lover. The taste of his mouth still burned on her lips. Now they were strangers again—aeons apart—separated by an abyss of suspicion and hostility. And she had no idea how to bridge the gulf—or if she should even try, she reminded herself painfully.

It was a crowded few hours. The police came, examined the damage, and found some tyre-marks that matched neither hers nor Adam's in a corner of the yard.

'Looks a bit personal to me,' one of them remarked. 'Got any enemies, miss?'

She did not look at Adam. 'Not that I know of. Except—I had a set-to with a man looking for antiques a few days ago,' she added hurriedly. 'And later some-one tried to break in. I did report it.'

'We know who you mean.' The policeman nodded. 'But he couldn't have done this because we picked him up on Bank Holiday Monday. Got into a house with alarms and a security camera,' he added with a chuckle.

'I see,' Tara said slowly, and with dismay.

'He didn't mention he'd been here, so we'll have another word with him,' the policeman went on. 'But we've got a puzzle here,' he added, pulling a face. 'Dif-ficult to see us getting a result over this.'

Later, a breakdown truck arrived and removed the car, the mechanic promising it would be ready the next day.'

With Adam silent at her side, Tara watched it go.

She said stiltedly, 'Thanks for all your help. But don't let me keep you any longer. I'm sure you have things of your own to do. People waiting for you.'

'I've come down here to work,' he said curtly. 'I'm going nowhere.'

'Oh.' She digested this. 'Are you—staying some-where local?'

'As local as it gets.' He nodded towards Dean's Mooring. 'I'm camping over there for a few days.'

'But how can you?' Tara protested. 'There's no elec-tricity—no water.'

'Sweet of you to be concerned.' His tone was deri-sive. 'But they were both connected earlier today, to-gether with the telephone. I need to have a good look at the interior—decide what structural alterations will be necessary.'

'Oh,' she said, touching the tip of her tongue to dry

lips. 'I—see.' She paused. 'You—you didn't bring Buster?'

'Not this trip. He's being looked after for me.'

'By Caroline, I suppose?' She kept her tone casual, hating the swift shaft of pain that transfixed her.

'Naturally.'

'Well—I hope this rain doesn't get any worse.' Now she sounded almost inane, she thought despairingly. 'I'm sure you'll find holes in the roof over there.'

'Then I'll just have to make sure they don't find me.' Adam bestowed a wintry smile on her, and departed.

Tara turned, with a silent sigh, and trailed back into the house.

Melusine jumped down from the dresser to greet her with a chirrup.

'Traitress,' Tara muttered as she bent to stroke her. 'Let's see what's left for supper.'

She felt too depressed and on edge to be really hungry, so she compromised with cheese on toast.

In a way, she wished it *had* been the so-called antiques dealer who'd slashed her tyres. She could have understood that. Now she had the worry of knowing there was someone else who actually wished her harm. X—the unknown factor, she thought.

It should have been comforting to look across at Dean's Mooring and see a light burning downstairs. But it wasn't. In some strange way it made Tara feel lonelier—more isolated than ever.

'Great,' she muttered, as thunder rumbled in the distance. 'That's all I need.'

She tried to settle down with her book, but Melusine, who hated storms too, kept prowling round, clearly spooked.

'Come on, baby.' Tara lifted her gently into her arms,

trying to subdue her own nervousness. 'Let's have an early night, and try to sleep through it.'

For a while this plan looked like it was working. The storm seemed to be receding, and Tara was just drifting into slumber, when the entire room was enveloped in sudden blue light and an almighty crash of thunder sounded directly overhead, shaking the whole house.

'Oh, God.' As Melusine yowled and shot under the bed Tara sat bolt upright, her mouth dry, her heart pounding as lightning flashed and the heavens roared again. She'd forgotten that storms could get trapped, circling endlessly, in river valleys.

I'm never going to sleep now, she thought, waiting for the next onslaught. I'll make myself some tea—see if that helps.

She got out of bed, slipping on her robe as she went out on to the landing and switched on the light. She was halfway down the stairs when the next flash came. She paused with a gasp, closing her eyes, waiting for the inevitable roll of thunder. When she opened her eyes again it was to find everything still pitch-black, with no friendly overhead bulb to show the way.

'Oh, no,' Tara groaned. 'Not the electricity. It can't do this to me.'

She waited for a moment, hoping it was just a temporary glitch, then cautiously began to feel her way down the rest of the stairs.

As she gained the hall she became aware of another noise making itself heard above the storm. A persistent knocking at the front door.

Her voice was tremulous. 'Who—is it?'

'Adam—open up.' His voice was curt.

'I'll have to find the key.' She ran her hands along

the wall until she reached the hook where it hung, then fumbled it somehow into the lock and undid the chain.

'Are you all right?' She was caught in the powerful beam of a torch, and put up a hand to shield her eyes. As Adam stepped in he brought the cool, clean smell of rain with him.

'Yes—but the storm's knocked the power out.'

'I saw your lights go off suddenly,' he said abruptly. 'That's why I came over.'

'You were—watching the house?' Her hand went to the lapels of her robe, pulling them together. 'Watching me?'

'Yes.'

There was something about his tone. She said, 'Something else has happened—hasn't it?'

'Perhaps. Probably nothing. I don't know...'

'Tell me.'

He sighed. 'I saw a car's lights coming down the track about an hour ago. I went out with the flashlight and it turned round and drove off.' He hesitated. 'I found that—odd, so I decided to—stand guard.'

'Oh, God.' Tara's hand flew to her mouth.

He swore softly. 'I knew I shouldn't have told you.'

'Yes,' she said. 'Yes, you should.' She paused. 'Did you see what kind of car it was?'

'I only caught a glimpse as it was turning. A big, dark saloon of some kind.' He took her by the shoulders, turning her firmly towards the kitchen. 'Let's have some coffee. Is there any brandy here?'

Her teeth were chattering. 'In the dining room. The sideboard.'

'We'll get some candles burning first, and the kettle on. With light, and a hot drink, it will all seem better.'

'I wish I could believe that.'

She sat in the rocking chair, listening to the storm hammering at the house and watching Adam in the candlelight. She felt cold, but it wasn't wholly through fear. Some of it was excitement, dangerous and illicit.

The coffee he made was strong, and judiciously laced with brandy. She felt the comfort of it penetrating down to her toes as she sipped.

She said, with a touch of constraint, 'This is—very kind of you.'

He shrugged, the lean face suddenly remote. 'When there's an emergency people have to pull together.' He paused. 'The worst of it seems to have passed.'

She said, 'Yes.' And, in a little rush, 'Do you think they'll come back? Whoever was in the car?'

'No.' Adam shook his head. 'They won't. Because they know you're not alone.'

She thought, But I will be...

She cupped her hands round the beaker. 'I wish Buster was here. I'd have asked you to let him stay with me.'

'I'm sorry,' he said. 'But I didn't know your riverside idyll was going to develop a sinister side.'

'Nor I.' She was silent for a moment, bending her head so that her hair swung protectively across her face. 'Adam—would you stay here tonight—please?'

'As a substitute for Buster?' he queried drily. The blue eyes rested on her thoughtfully, levelly. 'I don't think that's such a good idea.'

'I don't want to be by myself.' Her voice shook. 'I'm scared—and I've never felt that way before—not here.'

'The storm's nearly over,' he said quietly. 'The power will be back on soon, and the car may well have belonged to lovers desperate for privacy.'

'You don't really believe that. Or why would you have stood guard?'

'Because I'm crazy,' he said grimly. He paused for a moment, then sighed harshly. 'You win, Tara. I'll get a few things and come back.'

'I'll make up the bed in my parents' room.' She got to her feet.

'No need for that. I've a sleeping bag.'

'Then I'll get you some towels.' She looked at him, trying to smile. 'Adam—thanks.'

His mouth twisted. 'Let's get the night over with before we talk about gratitude.'

She was upstairs when he returned, a sleeping roll under one arm and a travel bag slung on his shoulder. He put the roll on the bed, glancing at the nightlight which she'd placed in a saucer on the bedside table. 'Every modern convenience.'

'Is there anything else you need?' She hovered in the doorway.

'Now there's a loaded question,' he drawled, then shook his head with sudden impatience. 'Go to bed, Tara. It'll soon be morning, then you'll have your car back and you can leave.'

He walked across to the window, thrusting the curtain aside and staring into the darkness, his back straight, his shoulders rigid.

She said quietly, 'Adam—you're still angry with me, and I don't blame you. I'm sorry I tore up your picture—said those things. I had no right...'

'It's not important.' His voice was crisp and he didn't look round. 'Anyway, I'd planned to give you the painting, so in a way you had the rights of ownership.'

'Oh.' That rocked her slightly. She swallowed. 'Well—goodnight.'

He turned then. His smile appeared to have been chiselled out of stone. 'I think that's too much to hope for—don't you? Now, off with you, and let's get what sleep we can.'

She trailed slowly across the passage and into her room. It seemed a lifetime since the storm had woken her, and the sheets felt chill and unwelcoming.

Still wearing her robe, she pulled the covers round her, then blew out her own nightlight.

She could hear Adam moving around, then the slight creak of the bed as it accepted his weight.

Far away, she heard the soft growl of the thunder, banished to a distance but still menacing.

Like my unknown enemy, she thought. And shivered in the darkness.

CHAPTER EIGHT

SHE was dreaming again, dark, lonely disturbing images that brought the salt, scalding taste of tears into her throat. She was running from hands that snatched at her, wading through deep streams where weeds twined round her, dragging her down into their treacherous depths. Making her moan in fear and negation.

She reached out—somewhere—somehow—in silent appeal, and found her hands taken, her body enfolded in sudden strength and comfort. Her cheek pillowed against the warm humanity of muscle and bone.

She tried to open heavy eyelids. 'Adam?'

'I'm here.' His voice was quiet and firm. 'Don't cry any more, darling. You're safe now. I've got you.'

She whispered his name again, and sank down on to a quiet ocean of complete peace.

Then woke quietly and contentedly to the first gleam of dawn and early birdsong. For a moment she lay still, savouring her new inner calm, then began slowly to change position, attempting to stretch sleep-languid muscles, only to find she couldn't move. That an iron weight seemed to be pinning her to the bed.

She looked over her shoulder, swallowing a gasp. Because part of last night's dream had become reality. Adam was there, lying asleep behind her, his arm tucked round her, holding her warmly and intimately into the curve of his body.

She'd never slept with a man like this before. Never been held so close, she realised with drowsy wonder, or woken in his arms. Even after sex Jack had always turned away, seeking his own space.

Common sense told her that she should do the same, and quickly. That sleeping with Adam might be one thing, but waking with him was another and more dangerous proposition.

She tried to release herself gently from his encircling arm, only to feel it tighten. A murmur of sleepy expostulation reached her ears. His lips brushed her hair, and she felt the warmth of his breath against her skin as he nuzzled the nape of her neck. Then, almost immediately, he was deeply asleep once more.

I'll wait a little while, thought Tara. Then I'll try again. Sighing, she closed her eyes, and drifted pleasurably away.

It was considerably later when she woke again, with hazy sunlight filtering through the curtains. And she was alone.

Tara sat up slowly, trying to fight down a ridiculous sense of disappointment.

Adam had left, presumably to spare her embarrassment, and she ought to be feeling grateful, not wistful, she told herself firmly.

She slid out of bed and went along the passage, only to be halted at the bathroom door by the sight of Adam, his hair damp from the shower, a towel draped round his hips, standing at the basin shaving.

He paused, and smiled at her. 'Good morning. Did you sleep well?'

'Er—yes.' She could feel the slow tide of colour rising from the soles of her feet to her hairline. She lifted her chin, determined to deal with the situation. 'I'm sorry about last night. About getting so scared. I'm not usually such a wimp.'

'I've never thought of you in such terms.' He was using the razor with long, clean strokes. She could, she realised with dismay, have watched him all day. 'But last night wasn't a one-off,' he went on conversationally. 'There's been fear in your eyes since the first time I saw you.'

Tara tried a scornful laugh. 'That's nonsense. What have I had to be afraid of—up to now?'

'That's what I mean to find out.' He rinsed his razor, then reapplied himself. 'But, at a guess, I'd say life,' he added almost casually.

'Indeed.' Tara straightened her shoulders. 'Well, I have to tell you that I have a terrific life—work I love, a supportive family, and my own home.'

'Every blessing,' he murmured.

'Exactly,' she said with emphasis. 'Last night, the combination of the storm and the possibility I was being—stalked threw me off balance, that's all.' She paused. 'So, I—I'm sorry for disturbing you.'

He shot her a swift, enigmatic glance. 'I think it's a little late to apologise for that—don't you?'

Her heart hammered against the cage of her chest. Nervously, she tightened the sash of her robe, a gesture clearly not lost on her companion, who raised an amused eyebrow.

'Is the power back on?' God, she sounded like a prim schoolgirl.

'Not yet.' He was grinning openly now, as if he'd read her thought, and she felt her body warm again self-consciously.

I really do need to be somewhere else, and fast, she told herself.

She said brightly, 'Well, I'll just go and let Melusine out.'

'I've already done so—and she's had some milk.'
Adam razed the last of the soap from his chin, and
splashed his face with water.

'Oh.' She paused. 'Then I'll make some coffee.'

He was drying his face and hands on another towel,
taking his time, his blue eyes conducting a leisurely
inspection of her—almost as if, she thought faintly, he
was committing her to memory.

'No,' he said casually. 'I don't think so.'

Tara heard herself swallow. 'Tea, then?' she ven-
tured.

He shook his head, smiling a little. 'No tea—no cran-
berry juice, apple juice or freshly squeezed orange either.' He flipped the handtowel back on the rail and
came towards her, halting a matter of inches away.

Tara stared up at him, her eyes dilating, her throat
tightening with something that should have been panic,
yet somehow wasn't...

She said, striving for normality, 'Nothing, then.'

His smile widened. 'On the contrary.' He reached
down and undid the sash of her robe. 'I meant to shave
and be back in bed before you woke,' he said softly.
'But maybe it's better this way.'

She felt the robe slip from her shoulders and pool at
her feet. And she let it happen, as if she were mesmerised.

Her voice was almost a croak. 'That's—silly. You—
don't shave before you go to bed.'

'You do if you care about your lady's skin.' His
fingers stroked her cheek, light as thistledown, then
teased their way down her throat to the delicate cleft
between her breasts. 'And I mean to be—infinitely
careful.'

He slipped his hands under the thin straps of her

nightgown, using them to pull her gently forward, and she came unresistingly, lifting her mouth to his as he bent towards her.

His lips were cool and fresh, exploring hers with a kind of exquisite, lingering deliberation. As he kissed her his hands moved, manipulating her nightgown straps so that the silken cups tautened over her breasts, tantalising them with the lightest of friction, bringing the rosy peaks to aching, delicious life.

She felt herself sigh against his mouth, a deep-drawn breath held for an eternity. As she descended into the sweet chaos of pure sensation she told herself, somehow, that she should hold back—walk away. That this was all wrong because Adam belonged to someone else, and it could only lead to heartbreak.

But, dear God, it was so long since she'd known what it was to be a woman. After Jack's betrayal, she'd believed herself armoured for ever against the seductive craving of the flesh, but it was only a fragile shell, after all, and soon shattered. All it had taken was Adam— *Adam*...

He lifted a hand and twined it in her hair, bending her backwards so his lips could caress her throat and the fragile hollows of her ear.

She could feel the heated hardness of him pressing against her through the thin layers of fabric which divided them, and instinctively her hips moved, thrusting forward in mute offering and acceptance.

'Wait.' The word was a teasing breath against her skin.

But there was no patience in her, only a need that had to be satisfied.

His breathing ragged, Adam hooked his thumbs under the narrow straps and eased them off her shoulders, sending her gown to join the robe on the floor.

'Oh, God,' he whispered, the blue eyes burning. 'I've dreamed of you like this. You filled my mind since that first evening, sleeping and waking. I even tried to paint you to—exorcise you—get you out of my system—but it was never any good.'

'I know.' Her smile was luminous. Gently, proudly she began to touch herself, as she'd done that day in front of the window. He'd seen her then only in his imagination—but he was watching now, his face stark with desire, heat flaring along his cheekbones.

'Tara.' Her name was torn hoarsely from his throat. 'What are you doing to me?'

She shook her head slowly, her gaze holding his, consumed in a mutual flame.

'I don't know,' she murmured. 'You tell me.' She reached out and loosened the towel round his hips. 'You—show me.'

Naked, he was magnificent, as she'd known he would be, and powerfully aroused. She felt her womanhood clench in excitement and anticipation.

Adam kicked the towel away and moved forwards to where she waited for him, lips parted breathlessly, eyes half closed.

He drew her slowly towards him until the tips of her breasts were brushing his chest. He began to feather tiny kisses on her face, while his hands smoothed their way down her back to the swell of her hips, then lower, to her slender flanks.

He lifted her effortlessly up against his body, and Tara slid her arms round his neck, her legs closing fiercely round him. He kissed her mouth hotly and urgently, then entered her with one deep, upward thrust.

Mouths clinging, they began to move together in pagan, instinctive rhythm. Almost at once Tara could feel the first stirrings of her climax beginning to build inside her, as if her body had been made for this moment alone and she was reaching the end of a journey started long ago.

Her hands gripped his damp shoulders. She tried to control her response a little—or it would be over too soon, and she wanted to keep the glory of him within her for a longer time.

'No,' he grated against the harshness of his breathing, as if she'd spoken aloud. 'Come for me, darling. Come now.'

Crying out soundlessly, she obeyed, her body convulsed by one sweet, dizzying contraction after another, wave upon wave of such savage beauty that she found herself laughing for sheer joy through the helpless tears that spilled down her face.

And heard Adam groan, his body shuddering violently as he reached his own culmination.

Spent, they sank, panting, to the tiled floor, and lay there still entwined in each other's arms.

'My sweet love,' Adam said huskily. 'I did not intend that.'

'Are you sorry it happened?' Tara touched the tip of her tongue to the column of his throat, savouring the musky male scent of him.

'No, witch, and you know that isn't what I meant.' He tilted up her face and kissed her softly. 'I wanted to take it slowly—make it good for you.' His mouth twisted wryly. 'Make it—memorable.'

'Oh, it was good,' she whispered. 'And I think I'll remember.'

'But I wanted it to be romantic, too. A long, sweet

seduction in a comfortable bed. Wine to drink afterwards.' He bent his head and kissed her breast, circling the nipple with his tongue, making it stand erect, then surveying his handiwork with a murmur of appreciation. 'I might even have peeled you a grape,' he added softly.

Tara, tingling from his caress, gave an elaborate sigh. 'So, I've missed out again. The story of my life.'

Adam smiled, and kissed her on the mouth. 'Not necessarily,' he whispered.

She had not known it was possible to feel so intensely—or so differently. This time Adam made her wait, bringing her over and over again to the edge of fulfilment and holding her there, in exquisite, erotic torment.

'Oh, please.' Her body twisted beneath his, seeking its release. 'Now—please.'

'Is this what you want?' He moved, paused, then moved again. 'Or—this?'

'You know.' Her voice was thick, almost strangled. 'You know—damn you.' And gasped as the first heady ripples of pleasure consumed her, lifted her to some undreamed of peak of ecstasy, then let her drift, trembling, down to some peaceful plateau where she could rest.

When she could speak, 'I never knew,' she said, her face half buried in his shoulder. 'I never knew how it could be.'

He stroked her flushed cheek. 'You weren't a virgin.' It was a statement, matter-of-fact, even tender.

'No.'

He was silent for a moment. 'Are you ready to talk about it?'

'About what?'

'About whoever it was made you look at the world through frightened eyes.'

Tara moved restively. Jack was an intrusion. An irrelevance. She shook her head. 'There's no one.'

'If you say so.' He lifted her hand to his lips, turned it over and kissed the palm.

'Do you know?' he whispered. 'Have you the least idea, my love, my sweet wanton witch, how lovely you are? How warm and infinitely willing?'

Only with you. She thought the words, but did not say them. Because they might imply she was asking for a commitment from him.

He dropped a kiss on her hair. 'I think we deserve that bottle of wine now. I'll get one.'

'No, I'll go.' Tara sat up, running a teasing finger down his chest. 'You stay there, and build up your strength.'

'Brave words.' Lying back against the pillows, he watched her through half-closed lids. 'If you have those kinds of plans, maybe we should do something practical, like eating.'

'Fine.' She reached for her crumpled robe. 'What would sir like for breakfast?'

Adam picked up his watch from the night table and inspected it. 'Better make that lunch.'

'My God.' She snatched it from him. 'Have we been in bed all morning?'

'You had something better to do?' He sent her a lazy grin.

'They were going to bring my car back,' she remembered belatedly.

'I think we'd have heard them,' Adam said drily. 'They'll want to be paid.'

'Yes,' she acknowledged reluctantly.

For a few hours, in Adam's arms, she'd forgotten everything. Now the real world was pushing its way back into her consciousness, and she wasn't sure she wanted it there.

I don't want to go downstairs, she thought, because I might find the girl I used to be waiting for me.

It was dawning on her that no amount of rapture could disguise reality, or make it go away. Quite apart from the ugliness that seemed to be threatening her, she realised that she and Adam still confronted each other over an unbridgeable gulf.

Their physical attunement could not be allowed to blind her to the fact that she found his plans for Dean's Mooring repugnant. Or that he was committed to another girl, whom he had now betrayed.

Just as Jack had betrayed her, she reminded herself, her throat tightening. No different. No more forgivable.

'What's the matter?' He was propped on an elbow, studying her frowningly.

'Nothing.' She forced a swift smile. 'I think the mention of food has made me realise how hungry I am. Will scrambled eggs do?'

'Perfect.' He smiled back, but his eyes were still watchful. 'Do I get room service?'

'I do charge extra for that.' She batted her eyelashes suggestively, clowning to hide her sudden emotional confusion.

'I'm sure we can negotiate a settlement to our mutual satisfaction,' he said solemnly, and Tara skipped out of the bedroom, laughing.

Just this day, she placated any hovering vengeful gods. I won't ask for more. I'll leave. He'll go back to his Caroline. And we'll never see each other again. That way, nobody gets hurt.

Or was it already too late for that? she wondered. Was this, in fact, the beginning of a pain that would haunt her through all eternity?

Curled up on the rocking chair, Melusine greeted her with a look of slit-eyed disapproval.

'How right you are,' Tara muttered as she prepared a tray with cutlery and two glasses, cut bread for toast, and whisked eggs in a bowl.

She was on her way back from the dining room with a bottle of wine when she heard the unmistakable sound of the back door closing, and footsteps crossing the flagged kitchen floor.

She froze, hands gripping the wine as if it was a lifeline. She tried to call Adam, but no sound would come.

'So you are here.' Becky, slim and chic in dark blue linen, appeared in the kitchen doorway. 'I wondered when I saw no car—and then found the back door unlocked,' she added chidingly. 'I know there's nothing worth stealing, but honestly, sweetie, I could have been *anybody*.'

'Yes.' Tara swallowed deeply. 'So you could. What on earth are you doing here?'

'And what on earth are you doing, lolling round in your dressing gown at this time of day?' Becky paused, her sharp eyes taking in the bottle of wine, then the tray for two waiting on the kitchen table. When she turned back she was grinning broadly. 'Well, darling, I see congratulations are in order.'

'It's not what you think,' Tara said, praying that Adam would not suddenly appear, stark naked.

Becky winked vulgarly. 'No, of course not.'

'There was a terrible storm last night,' Tara said with dignity. 'All the electricity went off, and some odd things have been happening. So—a neighbour kindly spent the night.'

'What neighbour?' Becky demanded sceptically. 'The ghost of old man Dean?' She clicked the kitchen light switch. 'No shortage of power now.'

'So I should hope.' Tara decided to change tack. 'Anyway, why are you here, Beck? Are the children with you?' *God forbid.*

'No, Ma-in-law, bless her, is collecting them from school and having them for the weekend. So, I thought I'd pay you a flying visit. Take a look at this mysterious boyfriend—neighbour—whatever.' She lowered her voice. 'Where've you got him? Tied hand and foot to the bed?'

To her fury, Tara found she was blushing hotly. 'Don't be absurd.'

'And don't you waste your opportunities,' Becky retorted, grinning. 'Use 'em, abuse 'em, and cast them aside like a worn-out shoe—that's my advice.' She eyed the bottle Tara was clutching. 'Are you planning to pour that wine?'

'Are you planning to drink and drive?' Tara riposted, stalking past her into the kitchen and picking up the corkscrew.

'One glass won't hurt me. And I have to drink a toast to your emancipation from the grisly past.' She shook her head as she seated herself at the kitchen table. 'Harry and I had begun to think it would never happen.'

'I'd be glad if you and Harry would mind your own business.' Tara removed the cork with restrained violence.

'No fun in that,' said Becky. She accepted the glass Tara handed to her and raised it. 'Here's to sex—the tonic that perks up every little bit of you. Long overdue in your case.' She eyed the mixing bowl. 'And crack another couple of eggs in there, darling. I'm ravenous.'

'It's all right,' Adam said calmly from the doorway. 'The lady can have mine.'

He was fully dressed, Tara saw with relief, and carrying his sleeping roll and bag.

'I really should be going.' The smile he sent Tara was friendly, no more, and his tone was casual. 'I'll take a rain check on lunch.'

'Are you sure?' She hoped she didn't sound as wistful as she felt. 'This is my sister, by the way. Becky Allan—meet Adam Barnard.'

'My goodness.' Becky's voice simmered with amusement as she gave Adam the full-blooded visual appreciation treatment. 'You're not a bit what I was expecting.' She shook her head. 'No indeed.'

'I see,' Adam said gravely. 'Is that a good thing or a bad?'

She laughed up at him, using her eyelashes outrageously. 'I'll let you know when Tara and I have had a little sibling chat.'

How many years would you get for strangling your only sister? Tara wondered savagely.

She tried to emulate Adam's casual note. 'Well—thanks for coming to my rescue last night.'

'Any time,' he said courteously. 'Just call and I'll be there.'

'Now there's an offer you can't refuse,' Becky murmured.

Tara gave her a fulminating look, and accompanied him to the front door.

'I'm so sorry,' she whispered miserably.

'Don't be.' His kiss was swift and hard. Instant melt-down. 'I'll see you later.'

'Don't you have any shame?' Tara demanded bitterly as she stormed back to the kitchen.

'Not much,' Becky admitted cheerfully. 'Never saw the need for it. But I'm seriously impressed with you, little sister. What a dark horse you are. How many more men have you got concealed round the place?'

Tara began to melt the butter for the eggs. 'What are you talking about?'

'Never mind. Keep your little secrets, if you must. But if you've made a choice, I'd have to say it's the right one.'

Tara bit her lip. 'There's no question of a choice. This is—not what you think.'

'No, of course not,' Becky said soothingly. 'He looks totally knackered, and you're like the cat that's got the cream. All quite normal.' She rose, glass in hand. 'And you're letting that butter get too brown,' she admonished. 'Cooking and lust don't mix, so why don't you leave lunch to me while you go and change out of the seduction gear?'

An unwilling laugh escaped Tara. 'Oh—all right. Anything you say.'

Washing and dressing restored some of her composure, and Becky's scrambled eggs, served with grilled tomatoes and crisp fingers of toast, did the rest.

Over lunch, she told her sister what had befallen her car, and Becky reacted with genuine shock.

'You've told the police, of course. What did they say?'

'They're not hopeful. No fingerprints and a partial tyre-mark.'

'But that's extraordinary,' Becky said slowly. 'I mean—why you?'

'That's what I've asked myself.' Tara shrugged. 'And so far I haven't come up with a solitary answer.'

'So when did Adam Barnard come into the picture?'

Tara took a sip of wine. 'He's Mr Dean's grandson. He owns the property.'

Becky whistled. 'Now there's a surprise. So the old boy wasn't a bachelor hermit after all.'

Tara expected a further barrage of questions, but Becky relapsed into pensive mode instead, rousing with a start when her sister began clearing the table.

'Well, I'd better be getting back.' She glanced at her watch. 'Just wanted to make sure your love life was running smoothly. As we've got the house to ourselves, I might welcome Harry home this evening in stilettos and a smile.'

'Invite me to the christening,' Tara said drily.

'Invite me to the wedding,' Becky came back smartly. She gave Tara a fierce hug. 'Bye, ducky. Come and stay soon—and bring the lover, whomsoever it happens to be at the time,' she added largely, and disappeared.

Or did she? It was at least half an hour later that Tara, from an upstairs window, saw her car driving off up the track.

No prizes for guessing where she's been, she thought wearily. She's incorrigible.

Adam arrived shortly afterwards.

'Hi.' Suddenly she felt oddly shy. 'Have you come for your glass of wine?'

He shook his head. 'I've been on to the garage and they've promised to get your car back here by four.'

'Oh.' She was taken aback. He was smiling at her,

but there was a veiled expression in his eyes. 'Well—there's no real hurry.'

'No?' he queried drily. 'I got the impression you were desperate to get away.'

Yes, she thought, but that was then...

She swallowed. 'I believe you've had a visitor.'

'The redoubtable Mrs Allan.' His grin widened appreciatively. 'Quite a girl, your sister. With a positive thirst for information.'

'Oh, God, I'm so sorry.' Tara bit her lip. 'She really shouldn't do this...'

'She cares about you,' Adam said flatly. 'And I told her nothing I didn't want her to know.'

'Did she ask about Dean's Mooring—what you were doing there?'

'Yes. We had a full and frank exchange of views.'

'I can imagine,' Tara muttered. She paused. 'I haven't much in the way of food left, so I don't know what we're going to do about dinner tonight.'

She was hoping he'd say, We'll go out somewhere—celebrate.

But he didn't.

'That's really what I came to tell you,' he said quietly. 'When I got back there were all sorts of messages on my answering machine. I'm going to be pretty tied up this evening.'

Tara looked past him. 'You're expecting visitors?'

'So it seems.' She knew by the hesitation in his voice exactly whom he was expecting. Caroline, she thought, and pain ripped through her.

He went on, 'And as I assumed you'd be hightailing it back to London...?'

'Yes,' she said, too quickly. 'Yes, of course. It makes absolute sense. There's nothing to keep me here.'

'Tara.' He took a step forwards and she took a step back, maintaining a careful distance between them. 'There's something I need to explain.'

'No,' she said. 'There isn't. Never apologise—never explain. Isn't that the new golden rule?'

'I'll take your word for it.' There was a touch of grimness in his voice. 'What I'm trying to say is that I'll be back in London myself next week, and I'd like to—keep in touch.'

She shook her head. 'I don't think so.'

'What the hell are you talking about?' he said roughly. 'Of course we're going to see each other.'

'Why?' she said. 'Because you took me to bed, Adam?' She shrugged. 'These things happen. It's not some world-shattering event. We had sex. It was terrific. You're great.' She kissed the tips of her fingers. 'The best I've ever had—believe me.'

'According to Becky,' he said quietly, 'there haven't been so damned many.'

She bit her lip again, tasting blood. 'I don't live in Becky's pocket, or she in mine. What does she know?'

'She seems reasonably well-informed.' He was drawling again, but his fists balled in the pockets of his jeans revealed he wasn't as calm as he seemed.

'Not that it makes the slightest difference.' Tara looked at him with cold directness. 'We went to bed together once. I don't intend it to become a habit.'

'And that's your final word on the subject?' His mouth twisted. 'We both know I could make you change your mind.' He stopped abruptly, grimacing. 'God—what arrogant crap. Please forget I said that.'

'Easily,' she said. 'Now, shall we both—get on with our lives?'

'Not like this.' He came towards her again. 'Darling, I need to hold you so badly—to make you understand.'

'No.' She held up a hand to halt him. 'What I gave this morning was given willingly—as you noticed. But that's finished. Over. Anything you want now you'll have to take—and live with the consequences.'

For a moment Adam stared at her in total disbelief, then his face hardened. 'So be it, then.'

Before Tara could move he took her by the shoulders, jerking her forwards into his arms, and his mouth possessed hers with a kind of icy ruthlessness.

She was being punished, and she knew it, but even his anger ignited a wild, shaking response, impossible to deny or conceal.

For one dizzy moment her breasts were crushed against the wall of his chest, and her thighs were slackening—parting, seeking the remembered hardness of his body.

Then she was free, one hand going mechanically to her plundered mouth.

The blue eyes swept her mercilessly—almost with contempt. 'Now sue me,' he said curtly. 'If you dare.'

CHAPTER NINE

IT SEEMED as if her car would never come back. She stood at the kitchen window, watching and waiting, her only regret that she couldn't simply walk out of this house that she'd loved so much, and escape.

After Adam's departure she'd packed everything. Even Melusine was confined in her cat basket, raging furiously.

'I'm sorry—I'm sorry,' she'd whispered as she fastened the straps. 'But this is the way it has to be. Because I've been such a fool. And now I have to run away.'

The car arrived in the yard at last, followed by the garage's pick-up truck. Tara paid the mechanics hurriedly, answered their questions about the police enquiries almost at random, and was transferring her bags and boxes to the boot before the pick-up had left the yard.

She'd just put Melusine in the car when she heard a dog barking happily.

Buster, she thought. So Caroline's here already—before I could leave.

Despising herself, she went back into the house and up into the room she'd used, the bed now stripped and the sheets and pillowcases washed and draped on a clothes horse in the kitchen.

Sheltered by the curtain, she peeped out. There was someone standing by the river, slim and tall, in a white dress, with blonde hair piled on top of her head and

Buster frisking adoringly round her. Tara couldn't see her face, but female instinct told her that the other woman was beautiful.

Chic, too, she thought, feeding her jealousy. Brittle, and no doubt expensive. A run-down house by a back-water would not be her world at all. Adam could pull it down and build a shopping mall, and she probably wouldn't lift a finger to stop him.

As she watched, Adam came into view. He walked to Caroline's side and put his arm round her, and she leaned her head against his shoulder.

But whatever I think they're a couple, Tara thought desolately. They belong together. I was a passing fancy, but she's what he wants and I have to live with that. Somehow.

Her throat aching with tears, she backed slowly away from the window and went downstairs to the car.

She hadn't been away for long, but her flat smelt unused—alien, she thought, wrinkling her nose critically as she bent to pick up her post.

Mostly bills and circulars by the look of it. The newsletter from her residents' association, a magazine subscription reminder, and a square white envelope addressed to her in handwritten block capitals. The same capitals straggled across the half-sheet of paper it contained. The message was short and to the point. The single word 'BITCH'.

She crumpled it in her hand, feeling sick. This weirdo knew where she lived as well as where she'd been spending her vacation. The car tyres weren't a one-off incident. Somehow she'd become a target.

She hardly dared play back the messages on her answering machine, but they seemed all right. Her parents had rung, and sounded wonderful. Becky had left a caustic message. 'Just checking, sweetie, that you really are away.' And Janet, her secretary, had rung, sounding flustered and quite unlike herself, needing to talk to her urgently.

Some problem with the report I left her? Tara wondered, mystified. Surely not. And she could always have asked one of the other associates for help if she'd needed to.

I'll sort it out on Monday morning, she thought, with a sigh.

And there was something else nagging away at the back of her mind, too, which she couldn't yet pinpoint exactly.

Is it any wonder? she thought with a shrug. It'll come to me eventually.

But, first and foremost, she had the weekend to get through. The weather was good, and she went out as much as possible; walking in the park, eating at pavement cafés, rather doggedly paying long-promised visits to museums.

And never, under any circumstances, thinking about Adam.

On Monday, she received a warm, if surprised, welcome back at Marchant Southern.

'Couldn't keep away from us, eh?' Leo Southern commented. 'Which is more than can be said for that secretary of yours,' he added with asperity.

Tara frowned. 'I saw she wasn't at her desk when I came in.'

'Nor likely to be, I'm afraid. She resigned last week and phoned in sick today, so I guess she won't be working her notice.'

'Janet's left?' Tara stared at him, dismayed. 'But why on earth should she do that?'

'She said she'd talk to you, but presumably she's thought better of that.' Leo frowned. 'I got the impression it was some personal problem—domestic crisis—boyfriend playing up—that kind of thing. She was a bit emotional.'

'Janet lives very happily with her mother, and as far as I know there is no boyfriend.' Tara sighed. 'I don't understand.'

She paused. 'Did you fill the slot at Bearcroft Holdings?'

'Yes, indeed, but not with the enterprising Mr Fortescue.' Leo frowned. 'Since we turned him down we've been picking up a few iffy reports about him on the grapevine. It's good you already had him taped.'

'I aim to please,' she said lightly.

'Hmm.' Leo scrutinised her for a moment. 'I can't say your break has done you much good, Tara. You look like a ghost.'

'I feel terrific.' She pretended to flex her muscles. 'Rarin' to go.'

'Well, maybe your first job should be finding a new secretary.'

'Not yet.' Tara shook her head. 'I'm going to find out why Janet wants to leave, and try to persuade her to change her mind.'

But although she rang Janet's home several times during the day there was no reply.

Maybe she really is sick, Tara thought, frowning. But why, then, doesn't her mother answer—unless she's ill too, of course? I'll phone again tomorrow, and if there's still no response I'll call round.

It wasn't a particularly strenuous day, but she felt

bone-weary as she let herself into the flat that evening. Melusine welcomed her with extravagant pleasure, and she attended to her needs before turning her attention to the day's mail. No square hand-written envelope this time, she noted with relief.

She'd done some basic food shopping on her way home, and she put some Debussy on the CD player while she prepared chicken with peppers, tomatoes and white wine for her evening meal.

It was all simmering nicely when the phone rang.

'Tara Lyndon speaking,' she said crisply, and the line went dead.

'Why don't people apologise when they mis-dial any more?' she asked the world at large on her way back to the kitchen.

She was slicing green beans when the phone rang again. This time, when she answered, she was greeted by total silence.

'Hello,' she said. 'Hello—is anyone there?'

She'd just convinced herself it was some technical fault when she became aware of a faint sound.

Someone breathing, she thought, her mouth suddenly dry.

'Look, who is this?' She tried to sound cool and in control.

But there was no answer. Just the breathing getting louder. Hoarse and stertorous, it seemed to fill her head, making her feel somehow—unclean.

'Who are you?' she whispered at last, her voice shaking. 'What do you want?'

'You'll find out—bitch!' A voice distorted, unrecognisable.

She wanted to put the phone back on its rest, but her hands were trembling too much. For a moment she thought she could hear her heart pounding, then realised it was someone knocking at the flat door.

Still clutching the phone, hand over the mouthpiece, she went to answer. Adam was standing on the doorstep, tight-lipped, his face strained.

As his lips parted to speak she shook her head, pointing silently at the phone she was holding.

He took it from her and stood for a moment, head bent, listening intently. Then he spoke, icily, briefly, succinctly and obscenely, before walking across the room and replacing the phone.

He looked at Tara. 'How long has this been going on?'

Her lips felt numb. 'Just since I got home this evening. 'I—thought it was a wrong number at first.'

'Keep thinking of it like that,' he said. 'A wrong number. A wrong mind.'

'Do you think it's the person who slashed my tyres?'

'I don't know,' he said. 'But from now on you get the phone company to monitor your calls. And you talk to the local police too.' He paused. 'Of course, it may not happen again.'

'What makes you say that?'

'Because he now thinks you're not on your own,' he said quietly.

'I'm sure he does.' She pushed her hair back from her face, aware of a sudden surge of relief at his intervention. And realising too how dangerous it was to feel like that. She hurried back into speech, trying to lighten the situation. 'But I'd say it's physically impossible—what you told him to do.'

He looked at her with the ghost of his old smile. 'Want to try it and see?' He saw her flinch, and put out a hand. 'No—that was crass—stupid. I'm sorry. Let's just say it's a good job I arrived when I did.'

'Yes,' she said. Then, more sharply. '*No*. I mean—why are you here? How did you find me?' She bit her lip. 'Oh, don't tell me. My beloved sister—who else?'

'Tell me,' he said. 'Why do you find it so hard to let people care about you?'

'No,' she said. 'Let me ask you something. How do your marriage plans stand at the moment?'

His mouth tightened. 'They've been put on hold.'

'I'm sorry. I thought you seemed—ideally suited.'

'I still think so,' he said. 'I shall just have to work on it.'

'And visiting me is part of the plan?' Her tone was angrily derisive. 'What do you want—a sworn promise that I'll never tell a soul about our little dance round the maypole? You have it—although I'm afraid Becky guessed, and she'll almost certainly have told Harry. So it can't just be our secret.'

'No,' he said. 'I already know that.'

She stared at him. 'Is this why your engagement's on hold? Because she's found out?'

'Yes, she knows,' he said abruptly. 'But that's not all of it. There are other factors.'

She swallowed. 'Adam—I'm sorry. I never intended this to happen.' She paused. 'Did you tell her?'

'I didn't have to.'

'Oh, God.' Tara sat down heavily on the sofa. 'That's—terrible. I—I feel so guilty.'

'You have no reason,' he said quietly. 'I made all the moves. The blame is mine entirely. And now I have to deal with it.'

Tara looked down at her bare hands, twisted together in her lap. She said, slowly, 'It may not be the end of everything. If you could talk to her—make her see it was a mistake—purely circumstantial—that it didn't mean anything.' She couldn't believe she was saying these things. 'She'll forgive you—I'm sure of it.'

'Could you forgive that great a sin?' His blue eyes were studying her with an odd intensity.

'Yes.' Her voice was almost a whisper. 'If I loved you. If I wanted to save what we had together.' She gestured awkwardly. 'They say sometimes it can make you—the relationship—stronger.'

'Do they?' There was a strange note in his voice. 'Well—I shall just have to see.'

He paused. 'Of course, in my case, there's an additional snag,' he continued. 'Because the truth is I still want you, Tara.'

His voice softened huskily—devastatingly. 'I want to hold you, and undress you. I want to kiss your breasts, and caress every inch of you, then lose myself in you and feel your body tremble as you come.'

'You—mustn't say that.' The words were torn from her.

'And the thought of having to exist for the rest of my life on memories,' Adam went on, as if she hadn't spoken, 'is driving me quietly out of my mind.'

Then choose, she screamed at him silently. Her or me. Because you can't have both.

'I said it was over,' she said from her parched throat. 'And I meant it. It should never have begun.'

She couldn't look at him—meet his gaze—in case he read her own hidden truth in her eyes. Because if he came across the room to her—if he touched her— she would be lost...

'No,' he said, with an odd bitterness. 'I'm starting to see that now—when it's too late.'

She was aware of him moving—walking away from her, and then the quiet closure of the door.

She sat for a long time, motionless and tearless, only rousing herself when Melusine jumped on to her lap, butting her head against Tara's arm for attention.

Tara picked her up and held her tightly.

'He's made his choice,' she whispered into the glossy fur. 'And now I'm the one left with the memories. Heaven help me.'

She'd hoped work might prove an anodyne. But she was wrong.

She went in and sat at her desk, but she couldn't concentrate. She'd just decided to call it a day when Leo put his head round the door.

'A new client,' he muttered. 'Asked for you particularly. Looking for a keen young architect to work towards a junior partnership in his company.'

And he stood back to allow Adam to precede him into the room.

'Miss Lyndon.' His smile was friendly, but impersonal. They might have been strangers meeting for the first time. 'Mr Southern tells me you have a gift for people.'

'Mr Southern exaggerates.' Tara studiously ignored his outstretched hand, and Leo's look of horror.

When they were alone, she said, 'What the hell do you think you're doing, Adam? Playing some new game?' She ticked them off on her fingers. 'We've had the friendship game—and the seduction game. Is this the business relationship game?'

'This is a serious enquiry. I want to recruit a new member to my team. I was told you offer this kind of service.'

'My goodness,' she said bitterly. 'Becky has been busy. Is there one single detail of my life you're not familiar with by now?'

'I don't know,' he said equably. 'Why don't you tell me about it yourself over dinner tonight, and we'll see if she's left anything out?'

She shook her head, her hands fiddling with the pen she was holding. 'We both know that's not going to happen.' She paused. 'Do you need someone to help with the Silver Creek development? I thought that was your baby.'

'Very much so.'

'I imagine you have your—Caroline's full backing for your plans? I mean she'd hardly want to live there herself.'

'I'm trying to reconcile her to the idea, though it's not easy. But I have her full support for what I'm planning to do there.' He leaned back in his chair, very much at ease while she felt wretchedly on edge. He was wearing a dark City suit today, with a dazzling white shirt and a silk tie in discreet jewel colours. He looked like serious money, and she could understand Leo's anguish at her cavalier reception of him.

She selected a printed form. 'Perhaps we could go through a few of your requirements—what qualifications you'd expect—range of experience—proposed salary structure.'

'My main requirement is for you to have dinner with me tonight. I need to talk to you.'

She dug her pen into the paper. 'Whatever you have to say, you can say now.'

'Very well.' He produced a scrap of paper from his pocket and handed it to her. 'Is this car number familiar?'

She glanced at it. 'No. Why?'

'Because it was parked opposite your apartment block when I left last night, and there was a man sitting in it. When he saw me looking at him, he drove off.'

'He probably thought you were going to clamp him.' She spoke lightly, but her heart was thumping.

'Tara,' he said quietly. 'We seem to be talking about someone who knows where you live—your phone number—and where you spend your leisure time. So where did he get this information? After all, you're not in the phone book.'

'You seem to have managed pretty well,' she said shortly. 'Perhaps Becky's been handing out my personal details to all and sundry.'

'You know better than that.' He paused. 'One of the reasons I came here today was to suggest you look more closely at your immediate circle, including your colleagues.'

Tara gasped. 'That's nonsense,' she said warmly. 'I know them all well, and there's no reason—' She halted abruptly as something occurred to her.

'Well?' Adam prompted.

She fidgeted with the papers in front of her. 'When I got back yesterday my secretary had left very suddenly, and no one seems to know why.'

'You'd been on good terms with her?'

'The best. I trusted her completely.' She spread her hands. 'I was even going round to see her, to persuade her to come back.'

'Did she know you'd be at Silver Creek?'

'No—no one did.' She paused, frowning. 'That's it—that's what's been nagging at me. Becky didn't know either—I made up some story to put her off the scent, but she turned up anyway.'

'And she wasn't expecting you to be with me,' Adam said slowly. 'She was joking about it afterwards, telling me how different I was from the image she'd formed.' His mouth tightened. 'I think you should call her, Tara.'

She nodded. Lifted the phone and dialled.

'Darling,' Becky carolled when she heard her voice. 'Are you still on Cloud Nine? I would be.'

'Beck, listen,' Tara said urgently. 'How did you know I'd be at Silver Creek?'

Becky laughed. 'Why, from the boyfriend, of course. The one you're keeping under wraps. He rang me in a terrible state because he was supposed to be joining you at the house and he'd lost the address and directions you'd given him.' She sighed gustily. 'You know what I'm like about directions. No wonder he didn't make it.'

'Did he say his name?' Tara felt hollow inside.

'Do you know, I can't remember?' Becky thought for a moment. 'Tell you what, though,' she added cheerfully, 'I'd stick to Adam like a limpet. Mystery Man sounded rather too charming for his own good. Smarmy, in fact. But maybe I'm being unfair.'

'No,' Tara said. 'No, you're not. I'll see you soon, love.'

She replaced the receiver and looked at Adam, swallowing. 'He rang her—spun her a story about joining me.'

'On a number he could have got from your database, presumably. If it was made available to him.'

'You think Janet—helped him?'

'Someone did.' His face was grim. 'Tara, if you're going to see her I'm coming with you, and no argument.'

She wanted to protest, to tell him she could handle it.

Instead, she heard herself say, 'Thank you,' as she reached for her bag.

Janet's house looked deserted, the door firmly closed, the curtains half drawn.

'I don't think there's anyone there,' Tara said as they walked up the path.

'I saw someone at the bedroom window.' Adam rang the bell. As they waited they could hear faint sounds of movement inside the house, but no one came to the door.

Tara bent and called softly through the letter box. 'Janet, it's Tara Lyndon. Please talk to me.'

There was another pause, then the front door opened slowly. Janet looked terrible. She'd clearly been crying, and her plump face was pale and strained.

'Oh, Miss Lyndon,' she whispered. 'Are you all right? I wanted to tell you—really I did—but he said he'd make me sorry—and Mum's here on her own all day—and I was so frightened.' She looked past them, her gaze flitting anxiously up and down the road. 'He's not there, is he? Sometimes he comes and sits in his car and watches the house.' She motioned them into the house. 'You'd better come in.'

'Who is he, Janet?' Adam asked gently. 'Who's been scaring you?'

Janet touched her dry lips with the tip of her tongue. 'Tom Fortescue,' she said.

As Tara gasped, Adam looked at her gravely. 'You know him?'

'He was a client,' she said tautly. 'He was hoping I'd recommend him for an important job. But I didn't.

There was something about him that didn't add up for me.'

'I thought he was so nice,' Janet said wretchedly. 'He came back after you'd gone, and asked me to have dinner with him. We had this lovely meal, and he said he wanted to see me again. That I was real—genuine.'

Tara took her hands and held them tightly. 'And so you are, love. Go on.'

'He rang me at work and asked me to meet him for lunch. But I waited for ages where he said, and he didn't come. When I went back to the office he was there—at my desk. He'd managed to get into the computer and made himself a copy of your report about him.'

She looked miserably at Tara. 'He said it was all right. That you'd helped him get this marvellous promotion and he wanted to keep the report as a memento. That he wanted to thank you in a special way. He was smiling and smiling, but I knew, deep down, that he didn't mean a word of it, because I knew what you'd said, and that he'd been turned down.'

She began to cry again. 'I said I'd tell Security what he'd done, and that's when he started to threaten me. He said he'd tell Marchant Southern that I'd helped him, and I'd be sacked. That I'd never work in any confidential capacity again. And Mum's only got her pension. She depends on my money...

'And then he started phoning me at home. He said he was going to teach you a lesson—give you more misery than you'd ever imagined. And if I tried to warn you, I'd be next. Wrecking your car was just for starters, he said.'

She looked piteously at Tara. 'I was at my wits' end. I just wanted to hide. I think he's crazy.'

'It's going to be all right,' Adam said, putting a firm hand on her shoulder. 'You don't have to worry any more.'

'And your job is still there for you,' Tara added. 'Take a few days off, and come back when you feel you can cope. And when we've dealt with Mr Fortescue,' she added grimly.

'And how are you, personally, going to deal with Mr Fortescue?' Adam asked as he frowningly watched her unlock her flat door a short time later.

'I don't have to,' Tara said briskly. 'It's a Marchant Southern matter now. I'll hand the whole thing over to Leo.'

'Will it be that easy?' His voice was disturbingly gentle. 'You've had a hell of a few days.'

Tom Fortescue, she thought, is the least of my troubles.

'The worst part was not knowing who it was—or why it was happening,' she said quietly. 'Now that I know, he's no longer a threat—just a sad, unpleasant creature. I can handle that.'

'Did it really never occur to you it might be him?' he asked curiously.

She shook her head. 'No—I'd just interviewed him, decided he wasn't—right in some way, and made my report accordingly. It was the last thing I did before I went on leave.'

And then I met you, she thought achingly. And falling in love drove every other coherent thought out of my head.

She turned, smiling resolutely. 'Well, thank you for your support. Once again, I'm—grateful.'

'Do I take that as my dismissal?' There was amusement in his voice, and something else, less easy to define.

Far better—safer—to say a bald yes and walk inside and shut the door. Instead, she heard herself saying 'Would you like some coffee?'

'I think we both need something,' he said drily. 'And I'd like to be sure your gallant words aren't just bravado.'

Tara busied herself with the percolator, listening to him talking softly to Melusine. It occurred to her, rawly, how at home he seemed in what, up to then, had been very much her personal space. Her throat muscles tightened.

'Do you want cream?' Keep it friendly, she thought. And practical. Forget the lover. Play the hostess.

'Black will be fine.'

He got up from the sofa to take the tray from her. She saw that he'd removed his jacket and tossed it over a nearby chair, and loosened his tie.

He said, 'I like what you've done with this room.'

Stupid to glow at his praise, she thought. 'I need some more pictures.'

'Ah,' he said lightly. 'I'll have to paint you another one. But this time without additions.'

She offered a constrained smile and poured the coffee.

As she handed him his beaker his fingers closed gently round her wrist.

'Relax, darling,' he said quietly. 'I'm not going to leap on you, however much I may want to.'

'Please don't say things like that. You have no right.' She kept her voice cool, and steady.

'No,' he said. 'You're perfectly correct. I—sometimes have difficulty—remembering, that's all.' He sighed, swiftly and harshly, as he released her. 'God what a mess I've made of everything.'

She drank some coffee. It tasted bitter and burned against her throat. 'Have you tried—talking to her? Explaining?'

'Yes,' he admitted tautly. 'But I can't seem to get through to her.'

'It may take time. You'll just have to be patient.' Tara bent her head. 'She must hate me.'

'No,' he said. 'I don't think she has it in her to hate anyone.'

'What a paragon.' The words escaped her before she could control them, and she winced at their bitchiness.

'No,' he said softly. 'I certainly wouldn't say that.' There was a note of tenderness in his voice that transcended even passion. He sounded like a man who'd found his woman and would fight to the death to get her back, and to keep her.

If Caroline couldn't hate, then Tara would have said she herself didn't have an envious bone in her body. But suddenly she knew differently.

Adam put his beaker down and leaned forward. 'Tara—I think we need to talk.'

'About Caroline?' She tensed, knowing she couldn't bear any more revelations. 'I think we've said enough...'

'No,' he said. 'About Jack.'

'Jack?' For a moment she stared at him in total bewilderment, unable even to remember who Jack was. Then, as her mind clicked into gear, hot colour rushed into her face. 'What has Becky been telling you?'

'Only some of it,' he said. 'I hoped you'd tell me the rest.'

'What is this—a mutual counselling session?' Tara

raked her hair back from her face with an angry, defensive hand.

'No,' he said. 'I just—need to know.'

'I'm sorry,' she said, tautly. 'But a couple of hours in bed doesn't give you the right to—pick over the bones of my life.' She stood up.

'I'm sorry,' he said. 'Our making love was a really terrible mistake, wasn't it?' The blue eyes looked up at her with a kind of anguish. 'But I wanted you so much, and I could have sworn you wanted me too. I knew it was wrong, but I thought I could make it right—somehow.'

'I think you'd better go.'

'May I stay?' he said. 'If I promise faithfully not to talk about anything personal?'

'You don't belong here,' she said stonily. 'You don't belong in my life.'

'Except,' he said softly, 'that we still have unfinished business—you and I.'

'I don't think so.' She shook her head.

'Oh, yes,' he said. 'You're going to find me an architect—remember. Fellow professionals—we can meet on that level, surely?'

'Why not?' She lifted her chin. 'It shouldn't take long. I'm very good at my job.'

'I,' he said gravely, 'could not even begin to list your many general and particular talents.'

He reached for his jacket, then paused, taking a flat square package from the pocket.

'I brought this for you. A memento of our brief association to replace the painting you tore up.' He paused. 'If you want to dump this too, I recommend the Serpentine.'

He walked across and put it into her unresisting hand.

'Goodnight, Tara.' He put a hand on her cheek, cupping the side of her jaw, letting his thumb stroke its vulnerable line.

She felt his touch reverberate along each nerve-ending and explode in every bone. As Adam lowered his head she lifted her face mutely to receive his kiss.

His mouth was achingly cool, breathlessly tender. And the hand that touched her face was trembling suddenly.

Take me, she screamed silently. Insanely.

She wanted to feel his hands on her breasts—parting her thighs. She yearned to fall with him to the softness of the carpet—draw him into her—know the velvet steel of his possession once more.

Adam lifted his head and stepped back. His smile was polite—the departing guest expressing thanks for a pleasant time.

'Call me,' he said, 'when you've drawn up a suitable short-list, and we'll talk. See you around.'

She had been standing, watching the closed door, for quite some time before she remembered the package she was holding. She tore off the wrapping, screwing it into a ball which Melusine pounded on joyfully.

It was a compact disc. 'Delius', she read. 'A Walk to the Paradise Garden'.

Only, she thought, there was no paradise. Not any more. Not ever. And her face crumpled like that of a hurt child.

CHAPTER TEN

LEO listened with obvious shock to all Tara had to tell him about Tom Fortescue.

'It all fits with the feedback I've been getting about him,' he said, frowning. 'People who've crossed him would suddenly find important files deleted from their computers, deals screwed up, whispering campaigns against them—all kinds of covert nastiness.

'But this time he's overreached himself. I suppose he got away with it so often he became arrogant—and careless,' he added coldly. 'But his luck's just run out. It's a police matter now. I presume Janet will be willing to make a statement?'

'I think so.' Tara sighed. 'I'm afraid she's been badly frightened—and hurt, too.'

'Bullies always pick on the vulnerable,' Leo said. 'Fact of life.' He eyed Tara narrowly. 'And you still don't look your usual vibrant self, my pet. Has this nonsense hit you that hard?'

Tara shrugged, and murmured something evasive.

'And Adam Barnard—what about him? Are we going to find him his architect?' His gaze became speculative. 'He asked for you personally, you know.'

'I'm a clever girl,' she said, secure in the knowledge that Leo would not recognise the underlying irony in her words.

'How did you meet him?'

'He has a place near my parents' house on the river.'

How simple that sounded, she thought, and how casual. And that was the way she had to see it. The way she had to reduce the situation to its essence. Then, maybe, she could learn to bear it.

'Have you met his partner?' Leo asked. 'Gorgeous creature.' He shook his head. 'If I wasn't an old married man...' He went off, chuckling, leaving Tara sitting rigidly in her chair, staring ahead of her.

Correction, she told herself, as pain slashed through her. It would be a cold day in hell before she could bear any of it.

Time went on. Days passed, and became weeks. Tara immersed herself in work, interviewing clients wanting to expand their workforce, and nervous hopefuls who needed to move onwards and upwards in their chosen fields.

Sometimes marrying one to the other was so easy, she thought. But finding someone for Adam was proving a problem—probably because she so badly wanted to get it right.

The short-list she'd assembled was sound, but it lacked some vital spark. She could happily recommend any of them, but she needed a star. She wanted Adam to tell her that she was the best—that she'd done a terrific job.

She'd almost given up hope when Charlie Haydon came to see her. He didn't have half the experience of some of the candidates, but he was almost touchingly keen, and his portfolio was slim but impressive.

'I joined an old-established firm because I thought that was the thing to do,' he confided. 'Trouble is they're not just established, they're rooted in concrete—and Seventies concrete at that. I'm getting nowhere, and I want to design good buildings. I know I can.'

When he'd gone, Tara added him to her short-list, and drew a small but perfectly formed star beside his name.

She rang Adam's work number, and was put through at once.

'Adam?' She kept her tone cool and crisp. 'I've got four people for you to interview. Three men, one girl, and I have a really good feeling about one of them. When would you like to interview?'

'The sooner the better, I think. Can you set something up for the beginning of next week?' To her relief, he sounded equally businesslike, although just the sound of his voice made her quiver inside.

'Yes, of course, although it may have to be spread over two days.'

'That's no problem.' He paused. Then, 'How are you now, Tara?'

'Oh—fine,' she lied brightly.

'Any news of Tom Fortescue?'

'Unfortunately, yes.' Tara bit her lip. 'The police went round to interview him and he lost it completely— tried to attack them. They arrested him, and his parents turned up to bail him out. Apparently he's always had problems, and had psychiatric treatment when he was a teenager. They thought he'd grown out of it. Now he's had some kind of breakdown and is in hospital.'

She sighed. 'Somehow I feel responsible.'

'No,' he said forcefully. 'Think of the threats he made, not just to you, but to Janet and her mother. He was stopped just in time. He was beginning to enjoy his own power. God knows what he might have felt justified in doing.'

She shuddered. 'Yes,' she said almost inaudibly. 'Yes, I know you're right.'

'Really?' There was sudden laughter in his voice. 'While I'm ahead, can I invite you to a party?'

'Adam...'

'It's strictly business,' he interrupted. 'It's to celebrate the relaunch of *Woman's Voice* magazine at the West Lane Hotel.'

'So why will you be there?'

'We designed their new offices in Docklands. I thought it might give you a chance to network,' he added silkily. 'Leo mentioned to me recently he was hoping to extend the firm's media base. I know he wants you to go.'

'Oh.' Tara gritted her teeth, realising she'd been ambushed. 'I see.'

'I'll get my secretary to fax you the details,' he went on. 'And I'll look forward to seeing you there.'

'Oh, *hell*,' Tara said stormily as she replaced her receiver.

There were phone calls from Becky to field, too. Her sister chatted airily about every subject under the sun—but never mentioned Adam. So clearly they'd been in contact, Tara thought broodingly, although her pride wouldn't allow her to ask outright.

She could always develop a last-minute illness, she told herself, as she zipped herself into her little black dress a few nights later.

If this party hadn't been hanging over her head she might have enjoyed her day. She'd been called by an ecstatic Charlie Haydon, telling her Adam had offered him the job, and two of her other recommendations had similarly good news to report.

But I don't have to stay, she consoled herself, as she tried to restore some *élan* to her pale face with blusher. I can call in briefly, do the rounds to keep Leo happy, then vanish.

She gave herself a last unhappy look in the mirror. She would have to do something to pull herself together—put her life back in order before her parents returned the following week, she thought. She couldn't present them with another emotional disaster.

She delayed as long as possible before taking a cab to the hotel. The party, she knew, was being held in the Park Suite, and it should be in full swing by now. Hopefully her arrival would pass unnoticed. Also her speedy and subsequent departure.

She was greeted by a hubbub of noise and a sea of people in which it would be easy to float for a few moments, she thought, taking up her position on the sidelines in an effort to be unobtrusive.

'Hi,' said an amused voice. 'You must be Tara.'

She found herself confronted by a lean brunette, with high cheekbones and smoky eyes.

'Yes,' she acknowledged. 'But I'm not sure...'

'Bernie—as in short for Bernadette—Vance,' the other girl introduced herself, pulling a face. 'I work with Adam. He told me to look out for you. I'd just about given you up,' she added candidly. 'But now you're here, have some champagne.'

She signalled to a waiter, and Tara accepted the glass she was given.

'So, you're the girl who pointed Charlie Haydon at us,' Bernie went on. 'I'm seriously impressed.'

'Thank you.' Tara sipped her champagne and tried not to look round the room for Adam.

'I've been told to introduce you to some people.'

Bernie stared about her. 'Now, where shall I start?' she mused. 'Emaciated model or advertising junkie—which would you prefer?'

Tara laughed in spite of herself.

'Neither, honestly. I'm sure you have better things to do than nursemaid me.'

'In other words, I walk away and let you do a runner.' Bernie shook her head. 'Adam would have my guts. He warned me you'd probably try it.'

'How nice,' Tara said too sweetly, 'to work with a man who's always right.'

'Better that than having to work with a man behaving like a bear with a sore head,' Bernie retorted vigorously. 'And that's what he's been like, believe me.' She grinned suddenly. 'But at least tonight there's someone in a worse state than he is. Caroline's got to make a speech presently, and she's dreading it. He's with her now, trying to calm her down.'

'Oh,' Tara felt hollow. 'I didn't know she'd be here.'

Bernie gave her an astonished look. 'I don't think she had much choice. She is the new editor of *Woman's Voice*, after all. This is her party.'

'I—see.' How could he be so cruel? Tara asked herself hotly. Putting us in the same room like this on such an important night for her.

She pinned on a bright smile. 'She's the editor and Adam designed the new offices. What a cosy arrangement.'

'Keeping it in the family, you mean?' Bernie shot her an amused glance. 'Sorry, but it wasn't like that at all. Caroline was approached for the editorial job quite a time after we were appointed. She was head-hunted, actually, much to her own surprise. I think she believed she was past it—which is nonsense, of course.'

'Of course,' Tara echoed. 'Oh, there's someone I know,' she fibbed. 'You don't mind if I go and speak to her?'

She walked away quickly before Bernie could think of an objection, hiding herself among the laughing, chatting groups, until a swift glance assured Tara that her minder had moved on.

And I shall do the same, she told herself, putting her empty glass on a table.

There was a stir at the far end of the room, and a ripple of applause, and Tara saw Adam come in, with a familiar blonde figure walking beside him, holding his arm.

So, it seemed he had been forgiven after all. And she should be glad about it. Glad that those few hours of temporary madness hadn't ruined more lives than her own. Only she wasn't. She couldn't be.

She turned away hurriedly, tasting the sudden scald of tears in her throat, colliding with someone as she did so, and muttering a hasty apology as she headed for the door.

'Tara.' A hand on her arm detained her. 'My God, it is you.'

Tara looked at the man confronting her, her lips parting in shocked disbelief. 'Jack?'

'No other.' His eyes appraised her. 'You look—successful.'

And you've put on weight, she thought, remembering the swarthy good looks which had once seemed so desirable. Now he simply looked—complacent, even smug.

She said, 'So you didn't stay in Brazil?'

'No, that didn't really pan out.' He shrugged. 'I've

been back for a while. I'm doing consultancy work—independent financial advice—that kind of thing.'

'Then why are you here?'

'Damned if I know, actually.' He shrugged again. 'When you're a spare man, all kinds of odd invitations turn up.' He laughed. 'So when this one arrived the other day I decided to accept with thanks. I've never been one to refuse free champers.'

The mass of people around them shifted, and, as if she was looking down a brightly lit tunnel, she saw Adam, standing alone, watching her. As their eyes met he raised his glass in an unsmiling toast, then turned away.

My God, she thought with bitter incredulity. So that's why Jack was invited. As my consolation prize.

When Adam was asking me if I could forgive someone being unfaithful to me, it was because Becky had told him about Jack—about what happened between us. He was trying to gauge my reaction if he brought us together again.

'Apart from the free champagne, I can't say this bash has much going for it,' Jack went on. 'And I gather there are going to be speeches. Why don't we go somewhere and have a real drink—fill in some of the gaps?'

In the first bitter days of betrayal Tara had fantasised about him saying those very words. Now, her impulse was to blast him out of sight.

Except that he was the lifeline that had been thrown to get her, with some dignity still intact, out of this room.

'Yes,' she said. 'Why don't we?' And saw his expression of self-approval deepen.

Bernie caught up with her at the door, her face ludicrously dismayed. 'Tara—you're not leaving. But Adam wants to introduce you to Caroline. Please wait.'

'So sorry, my dear.' Jack's tone was patronising. 'This lady and I have another engagement.'

She'd planned to dump him as soon as they got outside, but Jack had other ideas. Before she could speak, she found herself in a taxi with him, on her way to some bar he confidently assured her she would adore.

'Best margaritas in London,' he told her.

'I don't think I want anything else to drink, thanks,' she told him crisply. 'I have a headache.'

'Hair of the dog, darling. That's what you need.'

Had he always spoken in clichés? she wondered bitterly.

One drink, she thought, and then she'd go.

At the bar, which was a popular watering hole for City types, Jack ordered a margarita, but to his chagrin Tara insisted on an iced tonic water.

'Come on, darling,' he said impatiently. 'You don't have to play the Puritan with me.'

'This is all I want.'

'Oh, very well.' He picked up both glasses and took them to a corner table.

'So,' he said, as she unwillingly took the seat opposite to him. 'My lovely Tara—and not wearing any rings, I see,' he added, taking her hand and studying it. 'I thought Daddy would have married you off to some nice safe executive by now.'

'No,' she said, releasing herself, and fighting the impulse to wipe her fingers on her skirt. 'He lets me make my own choices—and my own mistakes.'

A more sensitive man might have twitched, but Jack's smile remained undimmed.

'So are you still beavering away industriously at Marchant Southern?'

'Yes,' she said. 'I'm an associate now.'

'An associate, eh?' he repeated with exaggerated admiration. 'There's posh.' He leaned towards her. 'You know, it's bloody amazing, running into you like this.'

Not, she thought, as amazing as you think. We were set up.

'I've often wondered what happened to you—how you were getting on.' He looked slightly uncomfortable. 'I even thought about calling you a couple of times, but I wasn't sure what reception I'd get. And now here we are.'

'Yes.' Tara sipped her tonic water, reflecting that her fictional headache was now a fact.

'So what were you doing at tonight's bash?' His eyes were curious.

Tara drank some more tonic. 'Showing the company flag.'

'Then maybe you should have hung on and met the amazing Caroline after all—although I don't think she'll need any help choosing her team,' he added, with a faint smirk. 'She's a formidable lady, even if she is a bit long in the tooth.'

'Long in the tooth?' Tara echoed, bewildered. 'What are you talking about?'

'About the new editor of *Woman's Voice*,' Jack said impatiently. 'People at the party were saying they'd thought the board would go for someone young and thrusting. No one could believe it when they appointed a woman who'll never see fifty again.

'Of course, she doesn't look her age, unless you get really close,' he added. 'But she gave herself away by having her son escort her. Everyone knows he's in his thirties.'

Tara touched the tip of her tongue to dry lips. 'Are you telling me that Caroline is—Adam Barnard's mother?'

'Didn't you know?' Jack gave her a pitying look. 'You weren't very well briefed, darling.' He frowned as she pushed back her chair. 'Where are you going? I thought we might go on to a club—make a night of it.' He gave her the smile that had once made her heart swoon. 'Catch up on old times. Invent a few tomorrows.'

She shook her head as she picked up her bag. 'No, Jack, thanks.' She gave him a swift, radiant smile. 'You see, the truth is—' she lowered her voice '—I wouldn't have you if you came gift-wrapped. But no hard feelings.'

She managed to pick up a cab right away, and asked to be taken back to the hotel. With luck, she thought, the party would still be in full swing, and she would see Adam—find out the truth for herself.

Her luck ran out a couple of minutes later as her driver braked. 'Bit of a jam up ahead,' he told her. 'Looks as if two cars have smacked each other.'

'Oh, no.' Tara bit her lip. 'Can we turn off—go another way?'

'Not in this traffic, love.' He switched off the meter, and they sat for twenty minutes until the collision was sorted out and the damaged cars moved.

'Still up for the West Lane Hotel?' the driver asked as he started the engine again.

'No,' she said. Even now the traffic seemed to be barely moving. And her confidence was fading too. Because, whatever Caroline's identity, Adam was still

going to be married to someone. He'd told her so. I
suppose if I was reconciled with Jack, I wouldn't be
on his conscience, she thought wretchedly.

'No,' she repeated. 'I think I'll just go home instead.'

As she mounted the stairs and rounded the corner of
the passage leading to the flat she saw a dark shape
sitting on the floor, leaning back against her front door.

For a moment she was frightened, then it unwound
itself and stood up, and became familiar.

She said incredulously, 'Adam? But what are you
doing here?'

'Waiting for you to come home.' His voice sounded
flat, and unutterably weary. 'I had to stay—to tell you
that however much you love him he's not right for you,
Tara. He'll never make you happy.

'I saw you with him—watched you leave with him—
and I thought I was going to die. I wanted to follow
you, to drag you back out of danger and keep you safe.

'And all the time I was thinking—if he's what she
really wants, if she loves him, and is prepared to forgive
him—then I'm going to have to find some way to live
with that.

'So, I thought I'd wait until you came back. Even if
you were gone all night, I'd be here when you returned.
And I'd talk to you—plead with you to change your
mind. Because the Jack Halstons of this world never
change. They're predators, always looking for the next
victim. And it broke my heart to think how unhappy
he could make you.'

'But you sent him to me.' She couldn't see his face
in the dimly lit passage, but she could hear the pain
and loneliness in his voice.

'Because you wouldn't tell me about him, and I

thought that must mean that you still cared—that you were still hurting. Maybe he was the only one who could put the light back in those frightened eyes of yours. I told myself you deserved to make that choice.'

He paused. 'Why did you go with him?'

'Because I couldn't bear to stay,' she said. 'And he was an excuse. Because I swore that I'd never let anyone hurt me again—and then found I didn't even know what pain was until I faced the emptiness of losing you.'

She threw her head back. 'I stopped caring about Jack a very long time ago, but I went on using his memory as a shield. Out of habit, I think. But when I met you, I realised you can't shut yourself away from life—from emotion. You have to risk the pain and accept the consequences. Or you're only half alive.'

She paused. 'Why didn't you tell me Caroline was your mother?'

'I meant to,' he said. 'I was going to—as soon as you took one step towards me, instead of two steps back. In the meantime it gave you someone to focus on. Stopped you asking awkward questions about the girl I was going to marry.'

His voice roughened. 'I knew from the first it wasn't going to be easy to get close to you. I was terrified if I pushed too hard—came on too strong—I might frighten you. That you might run from me, and I couldn't risk that.'

He shook his head. 'I thought if I could present myself to you just as a friend you might start to trust me. To like being with me.

'I swore I'd be patient—let you dictate the pace— and the terms—but you made it so difficult. I used to walk for miles with Buster, just to put some distance between us, but even then you were in my head every step of the way. My God, I used to fantasise about you naked like some adolescent. I used to look across at your house and imagine you there—at the window—waiting for me.'

She gave a little breathless laugh. 'You don't know how true your fantasy was. That's why I tore up your painting—because I thought you'd actually seen me and I was embarrassed.'

There was a silence, then he said carefully, 'I really wish I'd known that.' He paused. 'And I'd like to see you now, only the lighting out here makes it difficult.'

'Would you like to come in—for coffee?' She was shaking inside, half-joyful, half-scared. She unlocked the door and went in, switching on the lights.

Adam followed, taking her by the shoulders and turning her to face him, his blue eyes scanning her face with heated intensity.

He said, 'I love you, Tara. And I want you to be my wife. From the moment I saw you, hurtling through the front door in a fury, I knew you were the one. It was that simple.'

Her voice shook. 'Adam—this is crazy. You—you hardly know me.'

'Is that a fact? Then how is it I don't need to ask what your favourite colour is—or what books you read? The music you prefer? Because I already know. I've always known about you. You were implanted in my brain when I was born, and all I had to do was find you. And if we'd only met for an hour it wouldn't have changed a thing. Because you're my other half. My completion. So don't tell me it's too soon, my only love. We've wasted too much time already.'

He looked down at her searchingly—pleadingly. 'I'll

wait for you, Tara, if that's what it takes. Just as I did tonight, and for as long as you need. Only don't send me away this time.'

'No,' she said, and her lips trembled into a smile. 'Not again. Never again.'

He kissed her, and the world went away. They clung to each other, half-laughing, half-crying.

'We were going to have coffee,' she teased against his lips.

'No coffee,' he whispered back. 'No tea—or orange juice or any other damned thing. Just you—now and for always.'

They left a trail of clothing all the way to the bedroom. For a while they let themselves know the peace of lying in each other's arms, lovers no longer afraid to speak their love, or to look at each other. Able to smile without shadows.

He began to kiss her delicately, his lips brushing the wing of her eyebrow, the curve of her cheek, the pulse in her throat, and she felt her breathing quicken as the sweet, erotic tension began to build within her.

His hands were gentle as he began to love her, caressing her breasts, coaxing the rosy nipples to stand proud and firm under the subtle play of his fingers. He moulded the slenderness of her waist, showing her, with laughter in his eyes, how he could nearly span it with one hand, then lingered over the flat plane of her stomach and the graceful curve of her hips, before, finally, claiming the moist heated silk of her parted thighs.

Her body arched to meet him, the breath sighing from her throat as he touched her, the cool fingers stroking the tiny crest of her womanhood, creating slow tides of pure sensation, as if she was the sea and he the moon that drew her.

She moaned softly in delight, her hands seeking him in their turn, holding him, adoring the male power of him, then guiding him to her. Into her.

For a moment they were both still, as though acknowledging the miracle of their coming together. Then they began to move, their bodies creating their own intimate harmony, rising and falling, giving and receiving. Inciting, too, and withholding, balancing on some knife-edge of pleasure.

Until, at last, control became impossible, and there was only rapture.

A long time later Adam fetched wine, and they drank together out of the same glass, and talked softly about the life they would have together—and, with wonder, how impossible it had once seemed.

'I thought I'd lost you after I rushed you into bed,' Adam confessed. 'I hoped so badly that you'd tell me you loved me—but instead we were further apart than ever.'

She framed his face tenderly between her hands. 'I was just being noble. Handing you back to the woman you were promised to.'

'And all the time it was you.' He kissed the tip of her nose, then paused. 'Tara—if I'd told you that first night we had dinner together, what would you have said?'

'I don't know,' she told him honestly. 'I knew there was—something powerful there, but I'd spent a long time telling myself that love wasn't for me. Maybe I'd have stayed and listened. More probably I'd have run.'

She lifted herself on to an elbow. 'Where are we going to live?'

'I have a house in Hampstead,' he said. 'I thought you might look at it. See if you like it.'

'How big is it?'

'Big enough for two.' He smiled at her. 'Or more.'

She laughed, stretching luxuriously. 'Sounds ideal.'

'And for weekends we'll have Dean's Mooring,' he went on.

'But you were going to develop it...?'

'No,' he said. 'I abandoned that plan some time ago. Decided the place deserved another chance at family life. And I'm getting a lot of hassle from Bernie as a consequence. She saw it in commercial terms. I had to tell her my future happiness depended on it.'

'Oh,' Tara said, as light dawned. 'I see now. Bernie's your partner—your *business* partner.' She grinned. 'Well, Leo was right. She's certainly gorgeous.'

'Her husband and two sons obviously think so,' Adam said drily.

'Why did you change your mind—about Dean's Mooring?'

'Because of you,' he said. 'And because the ambience of the place had started to get to me, in spite of the past. I'd always thought of Dean's Mooring in terms of anger and unhappiness, and hated it. But being there with you made me see it didn't have to be like that.'

She said gently, 'Do you want to tell me about your grandfather?'

Adam lay back on the pillow, frowning a little. 'He was a very rich, very selfish man. He believed that women existed to serve, and treated my grandmother accordingly. And he was paranoid about people trying to cheat him, so they never entertained at home, or went out very much. But within the limits he imposed she made friends, and a life for herself.

'And when her daughter was born, she was determined that she should have independence. It was one of the few things she stood up to the old monster about.

'One day he announced he'd sold their house, and they were coming to live at Dean's Mooring. My grandmother was terribly distressed. It meant losing her friends, and the garden which she'd created and adored. And she was afraid, and rightly so, that it would mean Ambrose becoming more reclusive than ever.'

'What did your mother think?'

'She'd managed to distance herself. She'd gone away to school, and then won a place at university. She had her career planned, and she'd also met my father, who was doing post-graduate work.'

He paused. 'And then my grandmother died—very suddenly of a heart attack. When Caroline came home for the funeral my grandfather told her she was to leave university and live with him—to cook and keep house as her mother had done. And when she protested he got angry, and told her that she wouldn't be able to continue with her course anyway, because he was withdrawing all financial support.'

'What did she do?'

'They quarrelled—seriously. He said if she didn't do as he demanded he would never see her again. But she went back to university anyway. My father was doing paid research for one of his professors, and he had a full grant, so they got married and managed somehow.

'She wrote to Ambrose about her marriage, and told him when I was born too, but he never answered. And a long time later, when I was quite small, she took me down to Dean's Mooring. I can remember standing outside as she knocked on the door, begging him to open it. And his voice telling her to go away. That he never wanted to see her again, and as far as he was concerned she was dead.

'As we walked away I can remember her crying, and I promised myself then that I'd come back one day and tear the house down, brick by brick. Destroy it completely.'

He paused. 'The day you saw my mother was the first day she'd ever been back. She's been a widow for nearly five years now, and I knew she was going to find it—difficult. So I needed to be there for her.'

'Yes.' Her voice was soft. 'Oh, yes, of course, my love.' She was silent for a moment. 'We'll fight, you know.'

He dropped a kiss on her hair. 'Your cat, my dog. But the making-up will be more than worth it, I promise.' He looked at her, his eyes questioning, suddenly vulnerable. 'So, will you marry me, Tara, my one and only love?'

'I'm yours,' she said. 'Now and for always.' And drew him gently down to her.

EPILOGUE

As SHE leaned on the window-sill of her bedroom at Dean's Mooring, Tara could see that the leaves were falling from the silver birches across the river, and feel a tang of autumn in the late-afternoon breeze. The long summer was coming to an end at last.

It had been a busy sixteen months, with the wedding first, and then the renovation of the house to supervise. In fact, she and Adam had done a lot of the work themselves, until circumstances had forced her to take life rather more easily.

The sound of voices and soft laughter drifted up to her, and Tara looked down smiling as her mother and father came into view, with Caroline beside them pushing the baby buggy.

Strange how nervous she'd been of meeting Adam's mother, she thought. She'd watched with real trepidation as the tall, elegant figure with its immaculately coiffed blonde hair had walked into her flat with Adam for the first time. After all, this was one powerful lady.

But as Caroline had come close to her she'd seen that the impression of brittle chic was an illusion. That the still-beautiful face was warm and lived-in, and wise. And had found herself looking into eyes that smiled at her like Adam's.

'So you're going to be the daughter I always wanted,' Caroline had said softly, and hugged her.

And, after little Carrie was born, Tara had treasured with tears in her eyes the piece that Caroline had written in *Woman's Voice* on the joy of becoming a grand-mother and the beauty of her granddaughter.

She heard footsteps on the stair and Adam came in, carrying his daughter in the crook of his arm.

'She's starting to grizzle,' he announced.

'She knows it's suppertime.' Tara unbuttoned her dress and the baby's puckered rosebud mouth closed hungrily on her nipple.

Adam lounged on the bed, his face serious and tender as he watched them together. 'That,' he said softly, 'is something I shall never tire of seeing.'

Tara looked at him, her eyes luminous with love. 'You look pretty good yourself. Fatherhood suits you.'

'Marriage suits me,' he said. 'And you suit me most of all. Why have you closed your eyes?'

'Because I want to remember this moment always. The three of us here, and how safe we are, how loved and strong.' A smile quivered on her lips. 'Am I tempting fate?'

Adam shook his head. 'We make our own destinies. But whatever they throw at us in the future I'm going to be there for you, Tara.'

'And I for you,' she said gently. 'My dearest love.'